Femford School For Girls

Part One

by Ann Michelle

Please visit my website:
www.annemichellesworld.blogspot.com

TABLE OF CONTENTS

Introduction by Ann
—o—

Dear Readers,

I have always wanted to write a story like this. Just imagine... *somewhere out there*, there's a mysterious girl's school hidden away from the prying eyes of the public. This school teaches the daughters of the rich and famous the skills they need to become the leaders of tomorrow. But it also teaches another group of pupils. These students are here for a very different reason... whether they want to be or not.

This is the story of Lewis Stevens. Lewis stumbles upon the Femford School for Girls when he tries to figure out if his fiancée Maria is having an affair. Before he knows it, he finds himself enrolled at the Femford School. What's more, he quickly discovers that many of the other students are males just like himself! Why would anyone do this?! Can Lewis escape? Will he escape with his manhood intact?

This is the first book of two. I hope you enjoy it! Please leave a review and let me know what you think!

With love,
Ann :)

P.S. Thanks for signing up for my monthly newsletter. If you haven't signed up, you can do so here: https://annmichellebooks.wixsite.com/website. All you need is an email address. You won't regret it.

Prolog

—o—

Maria crossed her legs and let her five-inch white platform heel dangle from her soft tan toes. The white polish of her pedicure contrasted beautifully against her olive skin. She watched her shoe dance on the end of her big toe as she decided whether or not to tell her sister Vera what was on her mind.

"This is a lovely cafe," said Vera.

Maria nodded her head. "It's my favorite."

The two women sipped their drinks in silence for several seconds. It was clear to Vera that something was weighing on her sister. Not only had she called her here to talk, something she rarely ever did, but she seemed unwilling to talk about it now, which meant it was troubling her deeply.

"All right, tell me why I'm here," said Vera finally.

Maria sighed. "I'm quitting," she said.

"Really?"

Maria nodded her head. "I need to quit. The job is warping me. Do you know, I was looking through a catalog the other day and I saw these gorgeous designer slingbacks. Nothing unusual about that, right? Except, I started thinking, 'Gee, wouldn't Lewis look great in these?' *Lewis*, Vera."

Vera snickered. "He might look good in slingbacks? Give it a try."

Maria pursed her lips and shot her sister a disapproving glare. "That's not funny."

"Sorry."

"Seriously, why am I thinking about Lewis wearing women's clothes?" asked Maria unhappily. "I shouldn't be thinking like that. Lewis isn't like that. I don't want him to be either. Still, I keep having that thought, like my mind is stuck at the school and I want to see him in the school uniform."

"I know what you mean," said Vera. "Sometimes, I see Jay walking around in pants and flats and I think that it's unusual. 'Why is he out of uniform?' I wonder. And then I remember that I'm not at the school anymore."

"Flats?"

"What?"

"You said 'flats.'"

Vera blushed. "Sorry. I meant men's shoes. But like I said, all I can think of is that he's out of his uniform. You just get used to seeing them that way when you work at the school long enough."

"That's what worries me. And do you know the worst part? The worst part was when I told myself that Lewis would never wear women's clothes, I caught myself thinking that I could force him using the things I learned at the school. Can you imagine thinking that?" She sighed.

"It can be difficult to adjust."

Maria let out a cynical snicker. "Adjust? At least you don't think about paddling Jay back into his uniform."

Vera cracked a shy smile. She shook her leg excitedly. "Wanna hear a secret?"

"Sure," said Maria cautiously.

Vera's face flushed even more. She then leaned in closer to the table so she could whisper to her sister. "Jay likes it when I take charge. He's kind of let me take over. I've even paddled him a couple times when he disobeyed me."

"You did?" asked Maria incredulously.

Vera nodded her head. She had an uncontrollable grin on her face. She was wet too, though Maria had no way to know this. "He was so hard when I paddled him, I thought he might sprain his dick."

Both women giggled.

"Well, Lewis isn't like that," said Maria finally.

"I don't know. I'm starting to think all men are like that," countered Vera.

Maria shook her head. "See, that's again what I'm taking about. You and I both know that not all men are like that, but the longer I work at the school, the more ideas like that start to make sense to me. It's warping me. I should not being thinking about putting my fiancé over my knee to solve our disagreements whenever we argue... but I am." She picked up her drink and looked down into it, but didn't drink it. "It's almost become unnatural to see him trying to take charge of our relationship."

Vera nodded her head sympathetically. She had worked at the school before Maria for several years. She had even gotten Maria the job, and she knew that working their affected her view of the proper relationship between men and women, but it had made her more happy if anything.

"I do know what you mean," said Vera. "The longer you're in that kind of environment, the more it starts to seem normal. And if you're there long enough, the rest of the world starts to seem like the strange place. The thing is, it's not as bad as you think it is." She wanted to tell Maria that it was actually a good thing, but she knew that would be pushing too far at the moment.

Maria sipped her drink nervously. She didn't want a fiancé like *that*.

"So what are you going to do?" asked Vera.

"I need to quit. I need to get away from the school and back into the real world before I can't deal with normal men anymore."

"Sounds boring."

"Maybe, but it's what I need to do," said Maria.

"Have you told the Headmistress?"

Maria shook her head. "No. Not yet. I've got a contract for this term. I'm going to finish that and then give her my resignation and walk away. Then I'll marry Lewis and we'll live happily ever after a thousand miles away in another world."

Vera raised her glass in toast. She didn't want to tell her sister that it might not be that easy to get what she had seen and done out of her system. Some things become habits. Still, she wished her sister luck.

Chapter One: "Finding Femford"

—o—

Lewis Stevens watched his fiancée Maria pack her suitcase. She was going away to the boarding school where she taught. This would be her last term there. Then she would quit her job and they would get married when she returned. There was only one problem: Lewis had begun to suspect that Maria might be seeing someone else at the school.

"I wish you didn't have to go to that silly school," said Lewis.

"I know, darling, but I promised," replied Maria.

"Tell them you changed your mind."

Maria shook her head. "I have a contract, and these aren't the kind of people whose contracts you break."

"You always make them sound like Mafia or something. It's just a school. What are they going to do to you? Make you stand in the corner? Paddle you with a wooden ruler?" asked Lewis jokingly.

Maria tottered over to Lewis on her five-inch platform heels; she was a small woman and always wore heels to gain height. Even in her heels though, she barely saw eye to eye with Lewis, and he wasn't especially tall. To the contrary, he was on the short side for being a man. She wrapped her arms around his waist and kissed him.

"It won't be for long, darling. Just one semester. So don't get impatient. Don't make me stand *you* in the corner." She winked at Lewis as she said this, and he let out a laugh.

"That'll be the day!" he exclaimed. "If anyone gets put in the corner around here, it will be you." He playfully smacked her on the rear as he said this.

She wagged her finger at him in return.

"I want to come visit you," declared Lewis a moment later.

Maria stopped mid-pack as she was sticking a pile of panties into her suitcase. "You can't."

"Why not? I can stay in a nearby hotel. I won't be any bother. They'll barely even know I'm there. We can have dinner or something when you have free time," said Lewis.

"They don't allow that. I've told you this, Lewis," said Maria.

Indeed, she had. She had told him several times that the elite school where she taught simply did not allow visitors. That was their policy and they kept to it strictly and without explanation. The problem was, he wasn't sure he believed her. In fact, her unwillingness even to tell him where the school was located is what first raised his suspicions that she might be fooling around on him. Why else would she absolutely refuse to let him come see her? It was only a school!

This had been a matter of some tension from the first time she returned to school when they had just started dating. He had joked about the school being part of the CIA or some international school for assassins, but his joke was meant to hide his disappointment that she hadn't trusted him enough to tell him where it was.

Now that they were engaged and she still wouldn't tell him anything and wouldn't let him come see her, his disappointment had shifted to suspicious. Indeed, everything about the school bothered him now, especially the fact she wouldn't tell him anything about it. Just about the only thing she had told him was that it was a girl's school and that she taught comportment.

"Comportment?" he had asked.

"Yes, comportment."

"You mean like how to swish your butt around?"

Maria rolled her eyes. "Yes, that's our first lesson," she said sarcastically.

"Why am I picturing a room full of gangly rich girls tottering back and forth with copies of *Wealth of Nations* balanced on top of their heads?" asked Lewis.

Maria laughed. "Yes, Lewis, that's my classroom exactly."

"Why can't you tell me more?"

Maria sighed. "The school's clients are very private."

That was how all of his attempts to learn more ended... well, not this time.

This time, Lewis's curiosity level had been raised through the roof by her continuing secrecy. What could be so unusual about a girl's school that it required such secrecy? There was nothing he could think of. So there had to be some other reason, right? Well, what might be going on that Maria didn't want him knowing where the school was? When he asked himself that question, suddenly some very obvious answers appeared, and he didn't like any of them.

This question had eaten at him the last few weeks. By now, he could take it no more. So he put together a plan to find out what she might be hiding. This plan would help him find out exactly what was going on. It was a simple plan. It was an easy plan. It was a foolish plan.

—o—

They stood on the train platform. It was almost time. Lewis wrapped his arms around his diminutive fiancée and swayed gently back and forth. She squeezed him tightly and pushed her head into his shoulder.

"I'll miss you," she said.

"Do you really have to go?" he asked.

She sighed. "You know I do," she replied.

"I know."

Maria raised herself on tiptoe and kissed him on the lips. Their kiss lingered and lingered. Then they heard the conductor. Last call. The train was ready to leave. They hugged one more time. Maria broke their embrace. She took the final steps to the train and climbed the stairs into the car. She turned and blew a kiss before disappearing into the car. A moment later, the train began to move.

Lewis wasted no time. He walked over to the ticket office. He knew the train's ultimate destination was the coast, but Maria wasn't going that far. The problem was, he didn't know where else the train stopped. He did, however, know what she had paid for the ticket as he had seen the receipt... when he searched her purse.

"Hi, I was wondering if you could help me?" he asked the clerk.

She smiled indifferently.

He continued. "I just screwed up really badly. My boss just got on that train and I have a package I was supposed to give him before he left.

The problem is that I'm not sure where he's headed. I know he paid fifty-three seventy-eight for his ticket. Is there some way you can tell me what stop that gets him to?"

The clerk punched some numbers in her computer. "That would be Femford."

"Femford?" repeated Lewis.

"Yes, sir. It arrives at 2:10."

"Thank you. You're a life saver!"

Lewis raced outside to his car and punched "Femford" into his GPS. He was in luck. He had just enough time to get there before the train. He buckled his seatbelt and hit the road.

—o—

It was 2:05. Lewis sat outside the quaint train station in Femford. It reminded him of something from a 1930's novel about the English countryside. He decided to stay in his car because he could see the platform and the parking lot from here. It wasn't too busy either. That would help. If Maria got off the train here, he would see it. Then he could follow her.

"And I guess we'll see if she meets anyone," he told himself unhappily.

He felt sick to his stomach at that thought. He knew he was wrong to be here. He knew he was wrong not to trust Maria. But if she was having an affair, then he had to know... even if he knew he would rather not know.

"Ignorance can be bliss," he told himself.

He rejected this thought, however. He had to know.

Lewis watched the track.

After a few minutes, the train arrived. It was a sleek, modern train which seemed out of place at this quaint station. It stopped. Three people got off. About a dozen more milled around on the platform. No one seemed in any particular hurry. There was no sign of Maria.

Lewis began to wonder if he'd missed Maria or if this wasn't her destination after all. He debated going to the platform. But then she stepped off the train. Lewis recognized her immediately in her towering heels and her tight dark gray skirt suit. She stood out anywhere.

"All right, baby. Let's go see where this school is," said Lewis aloud inside his car.

She didn't move though. She just stood next to her suitcase.

"What are you waiting for?" asked Lewis.

As Lewis watched, a man drifted in her direction. Lewis tensed up. He told himself this could be the guy she was fooling around with! His stomach tightened into knots. He bit his lip.

The man drew even closer.

Maria seemed to smile at him or possibly

speak to him; Lewis couldn't tell at this distance. All he knew was that the man was walking right up to her. This could be the end of his engagement! But then, just as quickly as the man approached Maria, he walked past her and boarded the train. They hadn't even exchanged greetings. Lewis breathed a sigh of relief before feeling rather foolish.

A moment later, a woman in a black skirt suit and sharp black high heels approached Maria. They spoke briefly. Then another woman joined them. She had gotten off the train after Maria. She wore a white belted sheath dress and high-heeled sandals. All three women were gorgeous.

"The school sure knows how to find attractive women," Lewis told himself. He felt aroused.

The three women finished speaking and then disappeared into the station. They came out the front door about thirty seconds later and hailed a taxi. They climbed in and the taxi started toward the center of town. Lewis turned on his engine and followed them at a distance.

"Gotcha," said Lewis.

After about a mile up the main road, the taxi turned off onto a smaller road which led to a country lane. The taxi drove for maybe four or five miles along this country lane past farmers' fields until it came to a clearing and then a wooded area. About a hundred yards later, a large wrought-iron gate appeared between the trees and bracketed a dirt road which disappeared into the woods. Next to the gate was a large, decorative sign. The sign read:

Femford School For Girls
est. 1943
No admittance

As Lewis watched, the taxi drove through the open gate and vanished down the dirt road into the woods. He decided not to follow it at the moment because he didn't want Maria to see him. Instead, he would spend the night in Femford and then come back in the morning. He now knew the name of Maria's school and where it was. All he needed to do was come up with an excuse to get inside and look around. Then he could ask a few questions and get his answers. If he did it right, he could leave without Maria ever knowing he had been there.

Things would not turn out that way, however.

—o—

The following morning was a Monday.

Lewis had slept well at a little hotel near the edge of town. He arose and showered. Then he slipped into the gray suit and white dress shirt. He found that suits always brought instant respectability, which was useful at times like this when he needed to bluff his way into the school.

He packed his bag and made his way to his car. Then he drove to the Femford School for Girls. He easily found the gate again and drove right though. A few hundred feet ahead, he came upon a clearing in the woods. Inside that clearing sat a large building which looked a bit like something built for a French nobleman in the fourteen hundreds. Behind the building were two others. They were arranged like a triangle with a central courtyard. The buildings didn't quite touch, but dense hedges blocked anyone from entering the courtyard except through the buildings.

It was all very impressive.

"The school certainly has money," said Lewis beneath his breath.

Lewis pulled up before the door and stopped his car. There were two young women in dark blue dresses and high-heeled sandals standing near the stairs to the front door. They were chatting and giggling happily and paid no attention to him. He saw no one else. He wasn't sure what to do next, so he sat in his car for a moment before climbing out and starting toward the front steps. As he did, a woman in a black skirt suit appeared and came down the steps toward him. This could have been the same woman who picked up Maria.

"Can I help you?" asked the woman.

"Yeah, hi," said Lewis as he ran through his story one more time in his head. "I heard this was an amazing school, and I'm looking to enroll my daughter here next semester."

The woman raised an eyebrow. "Is that so?"

"Yeah. The thing is, I'd like to have a look around before I make up my mind."

The woman's face took on an expression that was somewhere between utter disbelief and amusement. It was almost as if she couldn't believe what she was hearing. Then her serious look returned. "Do you have an appointment?" she asked.

"No... I was in the area on business, and I thought I'd drop by."

The woman's face looked even more surprised. She seemed to consider this for a moment. Then she said, "Perhaps you should come inside and speak to the Headmistress."

Lewis smiled. "That would be perfect."

"What is your name?"

"Stevens. Lewis Stevens."

The woman motioned Lewis to follow her inside. She then turned and led Lewis up the stairs. As he passed the two beautiful young women, he nodded and offered a simple greeting. They both looked at him strangely, as if they were measuring him up for something, and then each giggle a "hello." This made Lewis surprisingly nervous somehow.

Lewis followed the woman in black down a long wide hallway. The hallway was sedately lit and had a lavish feel to it. The furniture was expensive and decorative, and there were ornate paintings of women all along the walls down the length of the hallway. Presumably this was to inspire the female students, or maybe it was old Headmistresses. Lewis didn't ask.

Again, there were girls in dark blue dresses here and there. Some sat on couches reading, others stood or sat in small groups chatting. Whenever he passed, they would all give him the same surveying look that had bothered him when he first arrived.

"I must make them nervous, being a man," he told himself.

That didn't quite sound right though.

Near the end of the hallway, the woman in black ducked into a large office. This was an administrative office and two women sat behind desks. They rose when the woman in black entered. Both wore simple sheath dresses to great effect. Indeed, so far Lewis was amazed at how beautiful the women were at this school.

"Stay here," said the woman in black.

She went into the office marked "Headmistress" and closed the door. She came out a minute or two later and summoned Lewis to enter. A moment later, Lewis stood in the office of Headmistress Angela Hunter. Angela Hunter was a small woman with a steely gaze that immediately made Lewis uneasy. This was not a woman he would want to be called before for discipline if he were a student!

"This is Mr. Stevens, Headmistress Hunter," said the woman in black.

"What can I do for you, Mr. Stevens?" asked Hunter. Her tone was polite, but it was clear she didn't want Lewis here.

"I'm looking for a good school for my daughter," said Lewis.

"And you thought that might be Femford?"

"Well, yes. Your school comes highly recommended. Everyone talks about what a great job you do."

Lewis had expected the compliment to help smooth things over and ease the tension in the room because people generally like to hear their accomplishments recognized. He was, therefore, surprised when a look of displeasure came over

Hunter's face.

"How much do you know about this school, Mr. Stevens?" asked Hunter.

"What do you mean?"

"Do you know what we do here? What our curriculum is?"

"Well, of course," replied Lewis, thinking that everyone knows what girl's schools teach. Heck, he even knew one specific class because of Maria. "You provide a basic education for young women. Math, reading, that sort of thing. You also teach things like, uh, comportment. That's why I'd like to enroll my daughter. I think she could use a school like Femford to prepare her. And I thought I would drop by to have a look around the school as I was in the area."

Hunter folded her arms and tapped the heel of her boot against the floor rhythmically. This made Lewis nervous and he bit his lip. Hunter definitely didn't seem to want him here. Apparently, Maria had been telling the truth about their aversion to outsiders.

At this point, Lewis was starting to worry. He knew his story wasn't a great one, but he thought it was enough. It was simple. It explained why he wanted to see the school and how he got here. What more could it need? *This was only a school*, even if it was private! Still, Hunter's reaction was making him nervous. She didn't seem to buy it for some reason.

"But what does she think I am then? A competitor?" he asked himself.

Lewis's mouth went dry. He glanced at the door and considered walking out right now before Hunter called the police or something. The last thing he wanted was a scene or something that might let Maria know he had been here.

Then Hunter took a deep breath.

Lewis tensed up.

"Would you like some tea, Mr. Stevens?" asked Hunter.

Lewis was surprised by the offer and he breathed a sigh of relief. He took this as a positive sign, that he had passed her test. He smiled politely and agreed; after all, he didn't want to rock the boat now by refusing her peace offering. So Hunter rose to her feet and walked across the room, where a tea service set sat on a cabinet. She poured out a cup for Lewis.

"Honestly, I'm just looking for a school for my daughter," said Lewis to fill the silence.

"Of course, you are," said Hunter.

"And I've heard this is one of the best."

"Where did you hear that, Mr. Stevens?" asked Hunter softly.

"Oh, everyone says it. I think I saw it in one of those national magazines too which rank schools," he lied.

A bemused look came upon Hunter's face. "How nice," she said. She brought the tea to Lewis and handed it to him. He drank it. It was rather sweet. When he finished, Hunter took the tea cup from him and set it on her desk.

"I suppose you'd like to have a look around now?" asked Hunter.

"If it wouldn't be too much trouble."

Hunter snickered. "It won't be any trouble at all, Mr. Stevens." She clicked her intercom button and summoned the woman in black. She appeared at the door a moment later. "Would you mind taking Mr. Stevens on a tour of the school, Miss Victoria?"

"Oh, I can show myself around," said Lewis.

Hunter smiled politely. "I don't think our lawyers would approve."

"Oh," said Lewis.

"It's all right, Mr. Stevens. Miss Victoria is an excellent guide."

Lewis rose to his feet and followed Miss Victoria to the door. An instant later, they slipped through the door and started off down the hallway. As they left her office, Hunter shook her head and sighed.

"Welcome to the Femford, *Ms.* Stevens."

—o—

Lewis followed Miss Victoria down some stairs and out a set of doors that led to the courtyard. The courtyard was triangular and ran about two hundred feet in each direction. It was crisscrossed by sidewalks and dotted with benches and oversized flower pots. The grass surrounding the sidewalks was perfectly maintained.

Scattered throughout the courtyard were perhaps two dozen young women in small groups. Most wore short white dresses, though a few wore matching dresses in navy blue. A couple wore dresses in a completely different style. Interestingly, each of these young women wore very high heels. This was the first hint Lewis had that something odd was going on here. Not that he disapproved of the fashion choice, but in his experience it was unusual to find so many women who were enthusiasts of spike heels all gathered together.

"I see the girls are all nicely dressed," said Lewis.

"Yes. We have a strict dress code," said Miss Victoria.

Lewis looked at several of the young women and smiled. Some of them were really quite stunning. Oddly, few seemed to return his smile.

Some gave him the same dismissive look he saw from the girls earlier and others seemed to look... for lack of a better word... *distressed*. Lewis suddenly felt queasy.

"Hot sun today," said Lewis. He was feeling hot now too.

"This way," said Miss Victoria and she turned from one sidewalk to another. A few dozen steps later, they entered what appeared to be a dormitory building. As they entered, Lewis saw an elegantly decorated common room occupied by several more young women in white dresses. They too work spike-heeled sandals.

"Everyone is wearing really high heels," said Lewis.

Miss Victoria ignored his comment and led him down the main hallway. As they went, Lewis's mind began to cloud over. He was starting to feel dizzy. He wasn't sure why. His queasiness grew too.

Halfway down the hallway, Miss Victoria opened the door to one of the rooms. The room looked more like something from a little girl's dollhouse than a room for a real person. The walls were covered in pink and white checkered wallpaper. The furniture was white and delicate. The bed had pink sheets and heart-shaped pillows. This had to be the room of a nine or ten year old girl.

"This is your room," said Miss Victoria.

"My room?" scoffed Lewis. "What? I don't need a room. I just wanted a look around."

Miss Victoria motioned for Lewis to enter the small bedroom. Lewis didn't budge. But then, a dizzy spell hit him and forced him to sit down on the edge of the bed so he didn't fall down.

"I don't— not my room— I— not staying. I'm— just school for— my daugh—"

"In that, Mr. Stevens, you are wrong."

Lewis looked up at the woman in black, but couldn't focus. There seemed to be three of her dancing in circles around each other. "Wh— what's— going on?" asked Lewis. He tried to stand up.

Everything went black.

Chapter Two: "Why Am I Dressed Like This?"

—o—

Lewis awoke in the same room where he had blacked out. He had no idea how long he had been out, but he knew what had happened. It all added up pretty quickly. Hunter had drugged his tea and Miss Victoria had left him here to sleep it off. The question was: why? What in the world would make her drug him? He had no idea. All he could think was that the school was a front for something criminal or Hunter and Victoria were crazy. Neither answer was comforting.

"I better get out of here while I can," he told himself quietly.

Lewis sat up and swung his legs over the edge of the bed.

"Whoa!" he exclaimed when he saw his legs.

Gone were his gray suit pants and his wingtips. In their place was... well... it was pretty incredible. The wingtips were replaced with high-heeled sandals. The heels of the shoes were really high. Lewis guessed they were about five-inches total counting the one-inch platform. That made these about as high as the heels Maria typically wore. The only difference was that these were wedges whereas she normally wore stilettos, though the difference meant nothing to him at this point.

His suit pants were replaced by silky tan stockings, which gave his naked legs a gorgeous feminine sheen. Beneath the stockings, it was clear that his legs had been shaved and all his hair was gone. And sticking out the front of the sandals, he could see that his toenails were each painted bright red. They made his feet look extremely feminine.

"What the hell!" he exclaimed despite himself. "That's not funny!"

He had no idea what to think. Why was he dressed like this? Why had they done this to him? Could it be a prank? No way. Drugging him was no prank. So could it be blackmail of some sort? Were there now twisted pictures of him seemingly partying with a penis in his mouth? Why would they do that? Who was he to them? Or worse, did this suggest that Hunter really was insane? That worried him.

"This could be bad," he told himself.

Lewis felt a growing need to flee this place. He threw off the blanket, intent on getting out of here immediately. That was when he discovered he was wearing a red leather corset and panties too.

"And that's really not funny," he said to the empty room.

He sat up and decided to strip off the corset. He searched for some latch or hook or zipper or something that would let him take it off – he now saw that his fingernails were long and red. He found nothing in the front. So he slipped his hands behind his back and felt for a zipper or laces or something. He found the laces, but wasn't able to untie them. There was no hook or zipper either. The corset would stay until he could cut it off or get someone to remove it for him.

"Doesn't matter. I need to get out of here."

Lewis jumped to his feet. Or at least, he tried. He managed to get his feet on the ground – his feet felt strange being held at a high angle by the heels as if he were standing on tiptoes. Still, he tossed his weight up off the bed as he normally did to stand. He even got his rear off the bed. But then the balance requirements of standing in thin high heels kicked in and he wobbled and almost turned his ankle and came crashing back down on the bed.

"This joke is wearing *very* thin," he growled.

Lewis placed his feet more carefully on the floor. He spread them wide apart and then slowly lifted himself to his feet. He managed to get himself standing, but he still wobbled and his ankles shook. Apparently, wearing heels was harder than it looked and he realized that running away in these would not be wise. He would likely fall and hurt himself and he couldn't outrun anyone who chased him.

"These things need to come off."

Lewis lowered himself to the bed again. He tried to push off one of the shoes with his foot, but it didn't budge. He looked down at the shoe to see why it hadn't come off. The shoes were sandals with several straps across the toes and over the instep and tight straps around his ankles. He would need to loosen the straps to remove the shoe. So he pulled one of his feet up into his lap so he could open the straps. He examined the straps until he found the buckle on the outside of the ankle. Unfortunately, there appeared to be a padlock threaded through the buckle and the strap locking the shoe into place.

"What the—?!"

Lewis pulled on the lock, but it was on there good and tight.

"How do I get these off?" he asked himself.

He yanked on the strap, but it didn't break. He pulled on the lock and the strap at the same time, but they didn't separate either. He even tried to stick his fingers inside the strap and twist the strap away from his foot, but that also did nothing. Like the corset, these things apparently were stuck until he could cut them off. He couldn't worry about that now though. Right now, he needed to get out of here before someone realized he was awake.

"I'm just going to have to try to walk in them," he told himself.

Once again, Lewis lifted himself to his feet. He pointed himself at the door and started toward it. He managed to take several decent steps, but nothing stable enough to give him any confidence that he could escape if chased. Still, he realized he had no choice.

"Maybe I can get better with some practice," he suddenly thought.

Lewis tried to pace back and forth across the room to get used to the heels, but that proved difficult and he really wasn't getting any better. What's more, his toes and arches began to hurt, and he decided to sit back down to give it one more try to remove the shoes.

The doorknob turned.

"Crap!" he said.

Lewis looked around for somewhere to hide or a way to flee, but there was nowhere and no way. He took a deep breath and waited tensely to see what happened next.

"Ah, you're awake, Mr. Stevens," said Headmistress Hunter. She entered the room with Miss Victoria and another woman following close behind. All three wore stiletto heels – boots for

Hunter – but Lewis knew this didn't level the playing field any for him. They could outrun him with ease and throw him to the ground any time they wanted.

"What do you want?!" demanded Lewis. "Why am I dressed like this?!"

"You wanted to enroll a student, now you have," said Hunter.

"Student? What student?! What are you talking about?!"

Hunter laughed ominously and sat down at the small desk that stood across from where Lewis sat on the bed. "I'm talking about you, Mr. Stevens. You are our newest student. Congratulations. It's not easy to become a student here."

This made no sense to Lewis. How could he be a student at a girl's school? He was leaning heavily toward the "crazy" theory now for Hunter. "Untie me!" he growled angrily.

"I'm sorry, Mr. Stevens, but your days of giving orders are over."

Lewis tried to stand up, but Miss Victoria easily pushed him back down onto the bed with a simple hand on his shoulder. In the heels, he could offer little resistance.

"Let me go!"

"No," said Hunter simply.

Lewis glared at Hunter. "This is illegal!

This is kidnapping! You can't do this to me!"

"I think you'll find that we can."

Hunter's calm tone worried Lewis. It meant that she had made up her mind and would not listen to reason. Whatever she had planned, she intended to see it through. "What do you want?" asked Lewis anxiously.

Hunter ignored his question. "Who do you work for, Mr. Stevens?"

Lewis furrowed his brow. "What?"

"Who do you work for?"

"That's none of your business."

"I thought at first you were a private investigator, come to investigate our little school. But I can find no record of you with any licensing agencies. Then I thought perhaps you were a journalist. But you don't strike me as that either," said Hunter. "So who are you?"

"I told you. I'm just here to enroll my daughter."

Hunter snickered. "*That*, you most definitely are not." She rose to her feet. "Well, we will find out eventually. And until we do, you will be our guest, going through our little program. Who knows... you might even like it?"

Lewis's worry was turning to fear. "I won't cooperate, you know that."

"I think you'll find you have no choice," said Hunter calmly. "Have you had a chance to take a look at yourself yet?"

"Yeah, very funny."

"Oh, I assure you, this is more than humor."

"Well, there's nothing here that won't wash off the minute I'm free. Nothing I can't take off."

"Is that so?" asked Hunter with a chuckle.

Lewis flipped the padlock on his shoe. "You think this lock will keep these on my feet?"

"That wasn't what I was referencing, Mr. Stevens."

At this comment, Miss Victoria came over and lifted Lewis to his feet. He was unstable and she steadied him. When he was steady, she slipped her hand inside the red panties he wore which matched the corset; he had thought nothing of them earlier as they didn't hinder his escape. She now yanked them down to the middle of his thighs. Lewis could do nothing to stop her because of his balance issue, but he instinctively dropped his hands to his crotch to cover his soon-to-be-exposed penis.

Only, it wasn't naked.

Lewis's penis was encased in a metal cage, with the exception of his testicles, which hung freely beneath it through a slot in the bottom of the cage. This slot surrounded the top of his scrotum as if it were a metal band wrapped around the scrotum sack. It was a tight fit.

"What the heck is that?!" gasped Lewis.

"That is known as a chastity device, Mr. Stevens. It is a way for a woman to keep her husband from having an affair by keeping his penis under lock and key. But in your case, I think it would be more accurate to call it a guarantor of obedience."

Lewis touched the cage. It was made of metal. It was shaped a bit like his penis too and he could see his penis safely tucked away inside it, where he couldn't touch it. He suddenly felt an intense desire to touch himself... to free himself. He grabbed the cage between his fingers and he pulled gently. It didn't move. So he pulled a little harder. He felt a tugging against the base of his penis and the top portion of his testicle sack, but still it didn't move. He was just about to give it a really hard tug when he wondered if that might not damage his scrotum or testicles.

"Problem?" asked Hunter with a sort of giggle.

"Take it off," he said.

"No."

"Take if off!" he said more loudly. His panic was creeping into his voice.

Hunter held up a small silver key. "Do you see this key, Mr. Stevens?"

"Yes," said Lewis.

"This key unlocks the reinforced metal bar

that has been placed around your penis and testicles. Without this key, the only way to remove the device would be to cut it with a rather large and rather imprecise metal cutter. The risks inherent in doing that should be obvious to you."

Lewis cringed at the thought of such a device working right against his skin and he imagined the chance of castration being unacceptable high. "Take it off!" he exclaimed.

Hunter continued. "This key will be given to your Mistress when your training is complete... not before."

"Training? What training? Mistress?"

"The training you will receive at this school. You will be trained to become a proper young lady, Mr. Stevens. A proper, submissive young lady."

Lewis furrowed his brow. "That's crazy."

Hunter smirked as if she knew something Lewis did not. Lewis swallowed hard. He knew there was no way she could turn him into a "submissive young lady." He wasn't worried about that. But she could definitely humiliate him in trying. In fact, looking at the way he was dressed suggested that she intended to embarrass him as much as possible. It also told him she was serious about making him go through the school's program, whatever that was.

"Ok, hold on. You said I only had to stay

until my 'Mistress' comes. Who is my Mistress?" asked Lewis.

Hunter shrugged her shoulders. "I'm sure someone will claim you."

Lewis suddenly realized what she meant. She meant that until someone came to unenroll him from the school, she intended to keep him here, going through the girl's school program... apparently even dressing the part. Unfortunately, no one knew he was here, so there was no one who could unenroll him.

"Now wait a minute," said Lewis. "What if no one comes?"

Hunter smiled coldly at him. "I'm sure someone will. Perhaps your employer will come rescue you. Then we'll know who you really for, won't we?"

"*No one sent me here*," insisted Lewis.

"For your sake, Mr. Stevens, let us hope that isn't true." She paused. "In any event, should you attempt to flee, you will do so without the key and without the possibility of removing the device. If that is acceptable to you, then by all means feel free to flee."

That actually didn't sound too good to Lewis. Still, it might come to that, he thought.

"But before you do," added Hunter, "let me explain one more detail of our obedience measures." She held up what appeared to be a fob for a car. "Do you know what this is? Or should I ask... do you know what this does?"

Lewis eyed the device suspiciously. "No," he said cautiously.

"Before we locked your penis safely away, we attached another device to it. Do you know what a shock collar is? Well, this is the same principle. Whenever I push this button," she said and she made her finger hover of a red button on the fob, "you will receive a strong, sharp shock. The longer I hold the button, the longer and greater the shock."

"You're joking!" gasped Lewis.

Hunter shook her head.

"You're threatening to shock me?!"

"Yes, Mr. Stevens. And make no mistake, if you disobey, it will happen. Every instructor in the school has one of these and is fully prepared to use it. What's more, should you try to escape, you will find that the device automatically issues a shock every three seconds when you pass out of range of our sensors, and it won't stop until you return back within range. The range is set for the grounds, no farther." She smiled coldly. "Think of it as an electronic fence."

"This is crazy!"

"And yet, this is your new reality."

Lewis shook his head. "But why? Why would you do this?"

Hunter folded her arms and stared at Lewis. "There are a great many people, Mr. Stevens, who will happily pay for the services we provide here. Some are wives wishing to remedy an injustice or undo a mistake. Some are mothers longing for a less unruly child. Some have other reasons. They pay us to do what you are about to receive for free—"

"But I don't want this! I don't want whatever you're doing here," protested Lewis.

"Whether you do or don't, these are the consequences of your trying to sneak into this school uninvited. I'm not sure what brought you here, Mr. Stevens, though we will find out... *rest assured*, but this is what happens to intruders. I will now leave you in the capable hands of Miss Victoria. Goodbye and good luck, Mr. Stevens... or should I say, *Laura*."

Lewis shuddered at being called by a feminine name. It was embarrassing. Even worse though, he cringed that Hunter seemed really to be doing this. She truly intended to make him attend a girl's school in drag!

"You can't do this to me," called Lewis after her as she left the room.

She didn't bother responding.

"What's going to happen to me?" asked Lewis to Miss Victoria.

"You're going to be educated."

—o—

Miss Victoria walked Lewis over to a large wardrobe that stood against the wall. The other woman stood nearby, apparently ready to assist as needed. When she opened the door, she revealed a collection of dresses and tops and skirts and shoes.

Lewis stared at the collection of feminine finery in horror. "No way!"

Miss Victoria chuckled and pulled out a white dress.

In the meantime, Lewis noticed the mirror hanging on the inside of the wardrobe door. This mirror gave him a good look at himself for the first time. He was shocked by what he saw. In those clothes, his whole body looked feminized. He had a roughly feminine shape and feminine legs. What's more, his eyebrow had been all but removed and now appeared high and arched and his hair had been dyed platinum blonde as well, giving him a quasi-feminine face. He wasn't passable as a woman – he looked like a man playing at being a woman, but parts of him had clearly been feminized.

"What have you done!" he gasped.

"We've only just begun, *Laura*."

Panic surged within him. Every fiber of his being told him he needed to escape this very minute. His body tensed. His hands balled into fists. He bared his teeth. He wasn't going to let Miss Victoria stop him.

"I'm leaving this asylum. Don't try to stop me," he growled.

He backed toward the door. He never made it.

Lewis felt the most unbelievable pain as a jolt of electricity passed through his testicles and his penis to his nerves and shot up his spine. For a moment, he thought his testicles had exploded. He grabbed them to make the pain stop. As he did, he lost his balance and fell to the floor, on his face.

"Oooooooooouch!!!!!" he wailed.

Then the pain stopped.

"A small demonstration," said Miss Victoria.

Lewis looked up and saw her holding the fob between her fingers. He still clung to his testicles which no longer stung, though the memory of the pain lingered and he wasn't willing to let them go yet.

"Would you like another?" asked Miss Victoria.

"No!" he gasped. "Please, don't!"

"Do we understand each other now?"

Lewis nodded his head pitifully.

"Very well. Then, from now on, you will

address me as 'Miss Victoria,' just as you will address the other women you meet as 'Miss.' And when I ask you a question, you will respond with 'yes, Ma'am' or 'no, Ma'am,' do you understand?"

Lewis nodded his head.

"What did I just say, Lewis?" asked Miss Victoria harshly. "Do you want another demonstration?" She held up the fob once more.

Lewis cringed. "No, Ma'am! I'm sorry. I understand, Ma'am! I do, Ma'am!"

"Good. Now get on all fours and kiss my foot to show your submission." As Miss Victoria said this, she raised her foot slightly and shook it to cause her shoe to slide off her foot. Then she moved her stocking-covered toes forward toward Lewis.

Lewis looked at her toes. He needed to kiss them. This was not something Lewis wanted to do, but he didn't want to feel that shock again either. It had been as if his testicles were going to burst; he never wanted to experience that again. So he reluctantly turned himself over until he was on his hands and knees. He crept forward a few inches until his face was near Miss Victoria's outstretched foot. He saw her red-painted nails beneath the silky stockings. He could smell the musky traces of sweat and leather coming from her foot. He felt sick.

"Go on," said Miss Victoria. "Do it."

Lewis closed his eyes and moved his face forward. He puckered his lips and planted a kiss on the top of her toes before pulling his lips away again as quickly as possible. This was disgusting.

"Now lick my toes," said Miss Victoria.

Lewis shot Miss Victoria an angry glance, which turned sheepish as he saw her finger move toward the big red button on the fob. He dove his face toward her feet and jammed his tongue onto her toes. He could taste the musky taste of old leather, the salty taste of sweat, the bitter taste of dirt and the sour taste of humiliation.

Something told him to get used to this.

Chapter Three: "Dodging A Bullet"
—o—

The next few minutes were a blur for Lewis. He already wore panties, the corset, stockings and the heels, but now Miss Victoria and the other woman added a very girly, very short white dress to the mix. The dress was white with navy-blue piping. It had a tight Peter-Pan collar, long tight sleeves, and an A-line shape, though it stopped mid-thigh. The dress was basic, yet felt professional or elegant. It came across somewhat as a uniform a young girl with a nanny might wear, and the word that came to Lewis's mind was "proper."

"This can't get any more humiliating!" thought Lewis.

They slipped the dress over his head and zipped it up in the back.

Lewis's humiliation grew. Adding this dress to the stockings and the high-heeled wedges gave a sense of the erotic to an otherwise girly look. He felt rather dirty wearing this.

"This is the new you, Laura," said Miss Victoria.

She then moved him before the mirror and let him examine himself. This was the first time Lewis's mind had a chance truly to grasp what he was wearing. He was wearing a dress and heels.

These women were seeing him in a dress and high heels. *He was dressed as a woman!* How humiliating!!! Up to now, he had focused so much on what was happening and how to escape that this fact hadn't really sunk in. Now it did and he blushed.

Then something strange happened... he grew hard within the device.

"What the—?!" exclaimed Lewis to himself. "How can I be getting hard?"

He didn't have an answer. He'd never cross-dressed before, nor had he done anything like this. Yet, he grew hard. He grew hard enough that his erection pushed against the confines of the cage and felt squeezed.

"I can't be excited by this," he told himself.

Fortunately, Miss Victoria didn't know. That would have made this unbearable.

"Now let's see if we can't help you walk a bit better," she said.

Lewis looked at the super-tall heels. "I'll never be able to walk in these things," countered Lewis.

"Oh nonsense! You'll be gliding along gracefully soon enough, Laura."

Lewis shuddered at the idea. What would his friends think if they ever saw him "gliding along gracefully" in high heels? They would mock him mercilessly, that was for sure.

"Over my dead body," he grumbled under his breath.

Miss Victoria moved the desk chair out of the way and then gave Lewis a quick tutorial in how to walk in the heels. She showed him the basics, gave him a few quick pointers, and had him practice for three or four minutes. This wasn't enough to make him entirely comfortable and it certainly wasn't enough to make him graceful in them, but it would let him walk without falling down. The rest, she told him, he would learn in class.

"What kind of class teaches walking in high heels?"

"Comportment."

All the color left Lewis's face. "Oh my God! Comportment? Isn't that Maria's class?!" A chill raced down his spine. The idea of being seen by his fiancée dressed like this horrified him.

"Come with us," said Miss Victoria.

Lewis's knees went weak. "Where are we going?"

"Start moving."

Lewis suddenly had a vision of himself surrounded by the other students as they laughed at him if he left this room... and what if they were headed to Comportment? This shook him and he found he could not move his feet. Then Miss Victoria flashed the fob and his fear of being shocked outweighed his fear of being seen dressed as he was. He reluctantly started moving. Only his utter horror at being shocked again gave him the strength he needed to take that first step, and each step toward the common area tested that resolve.

They stepped from the room. The hallway was empty. They started down the hall. Their heels echoed all around them: *CLICK! CRACK! CLICK! CRACK! CLICK! CRACK! CLICK! CRACK!*

Lewis's tension kept growing with each step. He knew he looked like a man in drag, not a young woman. He knew he would be spotted by the other students right away, and they would humiliate him.

"Can't we work something out?" asked Lewis nervously. His mouth was dry.

"I believe the time for that has passed."

They drew closer to the common area. Lewis felt incredibly nervous. He did not want to be seen! Yet, they kept moving down the hallway. *CLICK! CRACK! CLICK! CRACK! CLICK! CRACK! CLICK!*

"I promise I won't say anything to anyone about this school."

"I can assure you of that," said Miss Victoria.

CLICK! CRACK! CLICK! CRACK!

CLICK! CRACK!

"I swear. I won't say anything. Please, can't we reach a deal?"

She didn't respond.

CLICK! CRACK! CLICK! CRACK!

They stepped into the common area. Lewis braced for the shocked looks and the taunts he expected when an obviously cross-dressed man stepped into the midsts of these young women... but there were none. In fact, while there were around ten or twelve young women milling around in the common area, few bothered to look up and those that did returned to whatever they were doing without showing much interest.

Lewis was shocked. "Why aren't they freaking out?"

They walked right through the middle of the young women. Each of them looked up by this point, but none of them seemed to care. If anything, a look of sympathy appeared on their faces before they looked away.

"I don't get it? I'm a man... in a dress... *at a girl's school!*" he asked himself.

Miss Victoria didn't seem the least bit concerned either. She simply marched Lewis right past the other students and straight out into the courtyard, where it was mid-morning and sunny. She made no attempt to hide the fact he was a man.

There were more young women out in the courtyard. Some wore the white dresses, others wore the blue. The ones in blue struck Lewis as being more senior as they seemed to be leading the groups and the ones in white looked up to them. Of course, that was just a first impression. Oddly, it didn't seem to matter either if the ones in blue were younger than the ones in white. Either way, none of them were particularly interested in him. Lewis didn't understand this at all.

"You'd think they had cross-dressed men here all the time!" said Lewis in amazement.

Miss Victoria heard this and snickered. She then sped up, making it harder for Lewis to keep up with her. He had improved in the heels, but was still so unstable that any thought of escape immediately struck him as impossible; the ease with which Miss Victoria outpaced him confirmed that.

They started across the courtyard.

"Where are we going?" asked Lewis again.

"You're required to say, 'Ma'am,' when you address any member of staff... or any woman for that matter," said Miss Victoria.

Lewis's natural instinct was to tell her where she could stick it, but the image of the fob appeared in his mind and put an end to that. "Yes, Ma'am. Where are we going, Ma'am?"

"We're taking you for a check up before we begin classes."

"What kind of check up?" Again, he forgot the "Ma'am." Victoria displayed the fob and Lewis immediately got the message. "Ma'am! I'm sorry, Ma'am," he blurted out. He would need to be more careful.

"Next time, I won't remind you."

"Yes, Ma'am," said Lewis.

They continued in silence. Miss Victoria did not answer his question. It didn't matter though as he would find out where they were going a few minutes later either way, and it's not like he could have done anything to change what was coming anyways.

—o—

Lewis sat in a chair which looked suspiciously like a dentist's chair. The room was small with no view. It was clearly a medical room of some sort as it contained medical equipment. As he waited to find out what was going on, a tall blonde in a short nurse's dress and high-heeled sandals took his vitals and measured his height, weight and other physical measurements. She seemed most interested in the size of his chest and his hips and his biceps.

A moment later, a Rubenesque woman in a

white labcoat and thick heels entered the room. She took the chart from the nurse and read through the notes. She nodded her head approvingly.

"Everything looks good," said the woman in the labcoat.

"When can you insert the implant, doctor?" asked Miss Victoria.

Lewis tensed when he heard this. What implant? What were they planning to do to him? Would they really perform surgery of some sort on him without his permission? It seemed unthinkable, but then, look what they had already done. What was one more invasion?

"What kind of implant, Ma'am?" asked Lewis cautiously.

The woman in the labcoat smiled at him, but didn't answer. Instead, she answered Miss Victoria's question. "I can do it any time, but I'm wondering what course to follow." She showed the file to Miss Victoria and pointed to one blank line. "This concerns me."

"This is a special case," said Miss Victoria.

"I understand that, but without someone giving specific instructions, I'm not sure exactly what aesthetic result I'm supposed to achieve. Do I just take a guess or go with what I'd like to see? The possibilities are endless, but I need to know what the ultimate goal is. Can you speak to the

Headmistress please, and have her fill out the characteristics form?"

Miss Victoria considered this for a moment. Then she nodded her head. "Yes. I'll speak to the Headmistress and I'll get back to you."

The doctor smiled. "Good. Thank you." She then patted Lewis on the knee. "Until next time," she said.

Lewis breathed a sigh of relief. He seemed to have dodged a bullet... at least for now.

Chapter Four: "Lewis's First Class"

—o—

DOMESTIC DISCIPLINES: Students will learn how to perform basic domestic duties and to do so in ways that project the feminine image they are developing.

— Femford School For Girls Catalog,
p. 12.

Miss Victoria took Lewis from the small clinic to another room in the main building. They tapped their way down the tiled hallway in their high heels. Miss Victoria's heels echoed off the tiles with a sharp *CRACK* sound that sent tiny shivers racing through Lewis's body as his own heels made a more muted *THUDCLICK!* sound which made him feel foolish. This was not a sound men made.

As they made their way down the hallway, Lewis realized this wing of the building contained many classrooms, most of which were full of students. Some wore white dresses like himself, others wore the identical dresses in dark blue with white piping. Each was an attractive young woman, and he hoped none of them looked in his direction as he passed. For while none of the young women who had seen him so far seemed to react to seeing him, it was still super humiliating to be seen by any of these pretty young women dressed like this.

"Where are we going, Ma'am?" asked Lewis nervously as they pushed further into occupied territory.

"I'm taking you to your first class," said Miss Victoria.

Lewis stared at her incredulously. Was she serious? She was taking him *to a class*? A class where he would be surrounded in close contact by a group of these young women? Didn't she think that would be a problem? "Are you sure that's a good idea?" asked Lewis. "I mean, look at how I'm dressed."

"That is how the other students dress as well."

"Yes, but I'm a man... and anyone can see that I'm a man."

"And?" asked Miss Victoria.

Lewis was stunned. How could she not see the problem? He had seen himself in the mirror, he couldn't pass himself off as a woman. "What if these young women spot me?" asked Lewis pointedly. "And I will tell you that they *will* spot me. Then what happens?"

"Spot you?"

"*As a man!*"

"They know you're a man."

Lewis bit his tongue. Was she crazy? Did she not understand the significance of him being exposed as a man to these young women? Not only would it be humiliating, but it would be chaos. The young women would freak out and that freak out would spread like zombie plague or a wildfire until the whole school was in chaos. "Listen, Ma'am, I don't think you understand me. What is going to happen when all these young women figure out that the new girl is really a man? Shouldn't we try to hide that fact a little better? Or better yet, avoid it entirely?"

"You are here for school now, Laura. There is no avoiding it."

"But—"

"*As for giving it away*, your uniform indicates that you're male. That is the point to the uniform," said Miss Victoria coldly.

Lewis looked down at the dress he wore, which was now confirmed to be a uniform, as he suspected. How could a short white dress and high heels be a uniform that signifies he's a man? That didn't make any sense to him.

"Hold on—" said Lewis.

Before Lewis could say another word however, Miss Victoria pointed to an open door and moved him through it into a classroom. The room was maybe forty by forty with a row of windows which looked out onto the courtyard below; they were on the second floor. At the front of the room stood a woman in a calf-length brown skirt and a brown suit jacket with her dark hair tied back in a ponytail. She wore sand-colored pumps and tan stockings below her skirt.

Behind her stood eight young girls dressed exactly as he was in white uniform dresses and heels. Lewis snuck a glance at the students. He couldn't quite estimate what grade they were as some appeared older than others. They were all pretty though and he felt both ashamed and strangely naughty appearing before them dressed this way. His erection returned.

"Excuse me, Miss Susan," said Miss Victoria. "I have a new student for you."

"Oh good," said Miss Susan.

Miss Susan was older than Lewis and seemed quite spunky and enthusiastic. It struck Lewis that she enjoyed whatever she was teaching. He wondered how she would react though when she realized he was a man.

"This is Laura," said Miss Victoria. "He'll be staying with us for some time."

"Did she just refer to me as 'he'?" gasped Lewis to himself.

"Excellent," replied Miss Susan. "Welcome to Domestic Disciplines, Laura."

Lewis didn't know what to say. Had she not

heard Miss Victoria refer to him as male? Could she not see through the feeble disguise? Apparently not, so he said what he was required. "Uh... thank you... uh, Ma'am," he said.

Miss Susan glanced at him for several seconds as if she were expecting something more. When it didn't come, she looked to Miss Victoria, who nodded her head and responded, "He hasn't been taught to curtsey yet."

"Ah. I see. I'll add that to the list," said Miss Susan. "We'll get him sorted out."

Now Miss Susan had referred to him using a masculine pronoun! Lewis glanced at the other students expecting an avalanche of insults to begin, but they said nothing. They must have heard both women refer to him using masculine pronouns, why hadn't that surprised any of them? This confused Lewis. What was going on?

He didn't get time to think about it.

Miss Susan motioned Lewis and the others over to a corner of the room where a bed stood.

"Why is there a bed in a classroom?" wondered Lewis.

"Today, we learn to put on a bedsheet," said Miss Susan. She held up the sheet for all to see. "Making a bed properly will be something you will face every day. Not only your own bed, but other beds throughout the house will need to be made. It is vital that you know how to make a bed."

This struck Lewis as absurd. Why would a reputable private school teach its students to put on a bedsheet? He looked around to see if others felt the same way, but they all seemed to be paying a sort of nervous attention. "This place gets weirder all the time," he thought.

"Bambi, come forward," said Miss Susan.

"Ouch, unfortunate name," thought Lewis. "That's a name guaranteed that this young woman will never be taken seriously."

A young woman stepped from the crowd. She was quite attractive with soft, full lips, lush brunette hair, firm breasts and shapely legs. Lewis actually found her quite exciting and his erection stirred.

Meanwhile, Miss Susan was looking for another student to help with the demonstration. She settled on Lewis. "And why not our newest student as well," said Miss Susan.

"Me?" asked Lewis.

"Yes, you Laura. Please join Bambi across the bed on the opposite corner."

Lewis didn't want to draw any attention to himself, so he didn't really want to become part of this lesson, but he had no choice, not with that thing around his penis! He walked over the bed, still not gracefully in the heels, and took a corner of the sheet, as did the unfortunately named "Bambi."

"Do you think you can do this, Laura?" asked Miss Susan.

"Yes, Ma'am," said Lewis smugly. Who couldn't attach a sheet?

"Then you may begin."

Lewis separated the sheet until he found the corner. He pealed it apart despite his long red nails making this more difficult than it needed to be. Then he spread his legs to get better footing and he bent over and slipped the corner of the sheet over the corner of the mattress.

"Stop," said Miss Susan.

Lewis looked at her. "What's wrong?"

"That is not how you put on a sheet."

Lewis furrowed his brow. That was how he had always done it and he had never had any complaints. In fact, he'd never heard of there being a right way or a wrong way to put on a sheet so long as it ended up right on the mattress.

"Remove the sheet," said Miss Susan.

Lewis pulled the sheet off the corner of the bed and held it.

"Now stand next to the corner. Bring your feet together beneath you like this." Miss Susan demonstrated as she spoke by bringing her feet together so that her ankles touched. "Keep your knees together as you now give a slight knee bend." She motioned for the students to mimic her and they did.

Lewis found this simple pose to be rather difficult.

"Now bend at the waist, throwing your rear backwards slowly," said Miss Susan.

A sour expression appeared upon Lewis's face. He recognized the pose this would create. It was essentially a pinup pose of a young woman bending over, exposing her panties. "You're kidding," said Lewis.

Miss Susan glared at him. "Come here, Laura," she growled.

Lewis didn't move. To the contrary, he thought long and hard about making a break for it. Miss Susan wasn't nearly as formidable as Miss Victoria and maybe he could get away from her. But then he recalled the device on his penis and the pain it caused and the fact that any teacher could make it happen. And even if they didn't, there was still the "electronic fence." And thus he realized he had no choice but to obey. So he walked over to her and let her lead him to her desk.

"Grab the edge of the desk and spread your legs," said Miss Susan.

"Why?" asked Lewis cautiously.

Miss Susan pulled out a black fob. Lewis saw this and immediately grabbed the desk as instructed.

"I'm sorry, Ma'am," he said.

"Now hold that pose," said Miss Susan.

As Lewis watched, Miss Susan strutted over to the chalkboard. In the background, he saw the other students working with the bedsheet, putting themselves in the humiliating pose he had refused. Leaning against the chalkboard was a ruler. She picked it up and smacked it against her hand, giving Lewis a very clear idea of what she had in mind.

"You're not planning to—" started Lewis, but he never got to finish.

The ruler went up into the air and came crashing down on Lewis's rear before he could even react: *Crack!* It stung!

Lewis jumped forward and spun around, almost stumbling in the unfamiliar heels. "Stop!" he exclaimed and he pointed at Miss Susan.

"*Get back into position, Laura!*" growled Miss Susan.

"This is crazy!" exclaimed Lewis. "I'm sick of this!"

It took a second, that was all. Lewis felt his entire body catch fire and tighten as if he had been squeezed into a ball by a press. The unbelievable pain jolted through his testicles and his penis. He had felt this before but that experience had in no way prepared him for it this time. He crashed to the floor and grabbed his testicles where they hung out beneath the cage.

The pain stopped a second later, but it continued in his mind. He was defeated.

"You were saying?" said Miss Susan.

"I'm sorry, Ma'am," gasped Lewis through the memory of the pain. "I'll behave."

"I'm sure you will. Now stand up."

"Yes, Ma'am," said Lewis.

It took Lewis a moment, but he let go of his testicles and pulled his hands from beneath his panties. He got up onto his knees and then managed to stand in the heels. He knees were wobbly and the heels didn't help. When he reached his full height, he adjusted his panties and smoothed his dress.

"You owe the class an apology," said Miss Susan.

"Yes, Ma'am."

"When you give it, you will curtsey. Do you know what a curtsey is?"

Lewis had a vague idea, but not enough to say he did. "No, Ma'am," said Lewis.

"Very well. Stand tall with your feet and knees together," said Miss Susan. "Bend your head forward slightly, as if you are nodding. Grab the edges of your skirt between your thumb and first two fingers. Gently pull the skirt outward on both sides. Place your right foot behind your left foot. Shift your weight forward."

Lewis did as instructed and was overcome

with a feeling of submissiveness. He didn't like it.

"Now lower yourself about six to eight inches by bending your front knee," continued Miss Susan. "Keep your back straight as you do this and your head bent forward."

Lewis did this and felt even more submissive.

"Now hold that position for two seconds or until you are told you may rise. Then gently reverse what you have done until you are standing straight again," said Miss Susan.

Lewis finished the curtsey. He was so embarrassed.

"Now curtsey to the class. Then apologize. Then you may rise."

Lewis bit his lip. This had been rather embarrassing and it was going to be worse curtseying to this class of young women. They already knew he was a man... they had to know! Now they would see him humiliated like some sort of sissy. What must they think of him, he wondered. It couldn't be good.

Still, he was not going to defy Miss Susan.

"Yes, Ma'am," he said.

Lewis walked over to the assembled students who watched him with some curiosity, perhaps even a sense of private enjoyment at seeing another treated in some manner more humiliating than they felt humiliated themselves.

Their smirks made Lewis feel very small. He cleared his throat. Then he grabbed the sides of his dress, hung his head and lowered himself on his bended knee.

"I'm sorry for the way I acted," he said. He blushed bright, bright red.

Interestingly, as humiliating as this was, something about it made his penis grow hard. He didn't understand what could have caused it, but it definitely happened and that made this even more awkward. He was actually thankful it was trapped inside the cage at the moment.

"Nicely done, Laura," said Miss Susan.

"Thank you, Ma'am," said Lewis and he returned to his full height.

"From now on, you must curtsey when any teacher or guest walks into a room and when you are given a direct command from any teacher or female student. You are not to curtsey to any male students."

Lewis raised an eyebrow. "You have male students?" He had yet to see a single male anywhere.

"Of course."

"Where?"

Miss Susan looked doubtfully at him for a moment as if she wasn't sure if he was joking. Then she smirked and she let out a laugh. "They're the ones in white, darling. The young

women are wearing the blue uniforms."
Lewis's jaw dropped.

Chapter Five: "Girls and Boys"

—o—

After class, Lewis was returned to the dormitory to wait for lunch. The morning had been trying and humiliating... and now shocking. He had just come to terms with the incredible fact he had been taken prisoner and that they intended to dress him like a young woman – *turn him into a young woman* – when he now was told that this school of pretty young women was really a school full of transformed and transforming young men. Was that true?

"Is it even possible?" he kept asking himself as they marched him back to his sissy pink room.

Frankly, he wasn't sure he believed it. The other young women in his class looked like women. They really did. When he looked at them, he saw pretty faces, sexy curves, beautiful breasts, pouty lips, luscious hair, and feminine grace. They walked, talked and carried themselves like women. There was no trace of masculinity.

Moreover, he saw little difference between the young women in white and the young women in blue, except that the ones in blue seemed to be more dominant. Wouldn't that make *them* the men? Either way, they were both feminine and beautiful. How could one group be women and the other be men?

"None of this makes any sense," he told himself.

They reached his room and Lewis was sent inside. He was actually glad to get the break. He needed time to process this and what it meant. Could they really be males? What if they were? Did that change anything? Before, he had seen Hunter as just some crazy woman who somehow got her hands on a girl's school and now wanted to feminize him for some paranoid reason, but this changed everything. If she was really feminizing this many young men, then that was the true purpose of the school. She was intentionally feminizing young men!

What's more, someone had to be supplying these young men to her.

All of that meant he was in much greater danger than he realized.

"I really need to get out of here," he told himself.

He thought about the little clinic and the "implant" he avoided. That seemed truly ominous.

"I can't let them do that!"

But then his mind went immediately to the device. He needed to get that *THING* off his penis and these brutal heels off his feet so he could get out the front door to his car, assuming it was still there, and then as far away from here as possible.

"How do I do that though?"

He had no idea. Without the key, there seemed to be no way to remove the device. No sooner had he asked the question, however, than he was summoned from his room and he found himself lined up with a group of young women in white dresses... supposedly young men. They were then marched to the main building, where they would be fed lunch. His escaping planning would need to wait.

—o—

The lunch room was the largest room Lewis had seen yet. The room was probably a hundred feet across with floor to ceiling windows providing ample light. On the north side sat young women in blue at rectangular tables seating six students at a time. The young women in white sat on the south side – until he learned differently, Lewis refused to see the students in white as anything other than young women. In the middle stood a service area where half a dozen students in skimpy waitress uniforms were busy preparing meals and putting them on trays.

Lewis sat at one of the south-side tables with five other students from his dormitory. He knew none of the other students and didn't really want to know them. He preferred to remain as anonymous as possible. Still, he knew this was his best chance to speak to other students to find out what was really going on. Unfortunately, they seemed sheepish.

"Hey, I'm Lewis," said Lewis.

The other young men looked around nervously. None wanted to be the first to speak to him. Lewis took the opportunity to scan their faces for signs that they were male. He found nothing obvious; they all looked like young women. Finally, a young woman with long, blonde curly hair and red painted lips nodded in his direction.

"I'm Daisy," she said. Her voice was soft and feminine.

"I knew they were girls," Lewis told himself. He nodded back at her and repeated that he was Lewis. This seemed to open the door for the rest and soon introductions were made all around: Daisy, Bunny, Tiffany, and Cami. One young woman didn't speak, however. Lewis decided to push.

"I'm sorry, I didn't get your name," said Lewis.

"I didn't give it," said the young woman coldly. She looked away and shook her leg nervously, jiggling her high-heel encased foot.

"Don't mind him. He's just upset. That's

Edgar," said Daisy.

Lewis furrowed his brow. "Edgar?"

"Yeah. That's his real name too. His wife didn't change it."

"His wife?!" said Lewis incredulously. At the same time, he realized that Daisy had referred to "Edgar" twice using masculine pronouns. Had he found another man? He bit his lip. "So, um... is Edgar a... uh, um... male?"

This brought snickers all around. "Of course," said Bunny with a girlish laugh. "We all are."

Lewis swallowed hard. "You're *all* males?" he asked cautiously. "But your names— your bodies—"

"The names were given to us by our sponsors. We use them because it's too hard to switch back and forth and you won't get it right all the time. And if you don't get it right – one Will when it should have been Wilma – and they punish you. You'd be wise to remember that and use whatever name they gave you," said Daisy.

"As for our bodies," added Bunny, "we don't talk about that."

Lewis still struggled to believe any of this. These women were so beautiful, so feminine, so demure. They were shaped like women, sounded like women and even acted like women with the giggling and the sissy way they threw their hands about. How could they really be males?

"You're really telling the truth? You're telling me you're all really men?"

The others nodded their heads. Lewis looked them all up and down. Daisy was a looker with golden blonde hair. He had long delicate fingers with red-painted nails, a rather healthy chest, a narrow waist, a pointy little nose and a sweet feminine face. Bunny was more of the girl next door. Tiffany had the body and style of a fashion model. Cami looked like a delicate little girl. She was hardest to believe as really being a male beneath it all. Then there was Edgar. Edgar had exaggerated feminine traits. His lips were very puffy. His breasts were too big for his body, yet other parts of him remained stubbornly masculine. This didn't make him look like a man – none of them looked like men – but it gave him the look of an exaggerated woman.

"Why do you still have a male name?" asked Lewis of Edgar.

Edgar rolled his eyes, but didn't respond.

At this point, the serving girls brought trays for each of them. Each meal was a little different, which made Lewis think they were all on personalized diets, but all of it was either fruit or vegetable. There was no meat and no dessert.

"So why are you still Edgar?" asked Lewis again.

"It's his wife. She's trying to humiliate him," said Bunny softly.

"How does keeping a male name humiliate a man?"

"Think about it. After all the other changes she's making, Edgar won't be able to pass as a man anymore, right? His best bet to avoid a world of humiliation will be to hide as a woman. But how can he do that if his name is 'Edgar'?"

Lewis shuddered at the thought of the humiliation Edgar would endure introducing himself as "Edgar." He instantly wondered how Edgar's wife could be so cruel. "Can you pick a different name?"

Edgar shook his head, but Bunny answered. "No. Each student's sponsor picks their name. Do you really think I would pick 'Bunny' if I was going to give myself a girl's name?"

"Their sponsor?"

"Yeah. Whoever signed you up? For Edgar, that's his wife. She enrolled him."

"Your wife enrolled you?" gasped Lewis.

"Yeah, but don't let him kid you," said Cami with a cynical snicker. "He's the only one of us who *wants* to be here. Isn't that right, girls?"

"Don't call me 'girl'," said Daisy.

"It'll be true soon enough."

Lewis ignored this exchange. He was stunned to hear that Edgar actually wanted to be here. "You really *want* to be here?" he asked incredulously.

Edgar waved his hand dismissively with their pretty French tipped nails.

"You know, I don't understand any of this," said Lewis. "Is everyone here a man?"

"Not everyone," said Tiffany. His voice was far too high and small to belong to a man. Lewis's doubt returned and he wondered if they weren't all having some massive joke at his expense.

"Not as many as when we got here either," said Cami.

The others seemed to cringe at this statement and then intentionally ignored it. Tiffany continued by motioning toward the students in the dark blue dresses across the great room. "They aren't," he said.

"What are they?"

"Women... girls."

"Real girls?"

The others nodded their heads.

"So this really is a girl's school?" asked Lewis.

"In a way," said Cami. He ran his fingers through his hair as a nervous reflex. "The girls over there go through a regular curriculum for a girl's school. So in that respect, it's a normal girl's school. They also go through what they call 'The Leadership Program,' which teaches them to be more dominant."

"Dominant?"

"Yes. They learn to control men."

"We, on the other hand," interjected Edgar, "go through a very different type of training."

Lewis nodded his head bitterly. "I know. I had my first Domestic Disciplines class today."

Several of the feminized young men giggled. "You've barely scratched the surface," said Tiffany.

"It gets worse?" asked Lewis.

"It gets worse," said Edgar.

"Conversational etiquette," said Bunny.

"Comportment," added Daisy.

"Obedience," said Cami.

"Demasculinization," said Tiffany. She said this slowly and with emphasis, which made the others cringe.

"The point is," said Daisy to keep the others from running too far a field and turning the conversation into a shambles, "it's going to get a lot worse. And then there are the other changes," said Daisy.

"What changes?" asked Lewis.

"That depends on your sponsor."

"I don't have a sponsor," said Lewis. "I'm here... kind of by accident."

The others glanced at each other uncertainly upon hearing this. This was new information in their world and they didn't know how to handle new information too well these days. It gave them a sense that they weren't yet fully aware of all the terrible secrets this place held. So they became strangely silent. Lewis could sense their embarrassment and discomfort.

"How did you end up here?" asked Lewis to change the topic.

"It's complicated," said Daisy.

"Complicated how?" asked Lewis.

Daisy took a deep breath and twisted his rose-red lips. There was something oddly cute about this pensive look, which actually turned Lewis on. Lewis would have been bothered by finding himself excited at watching a feminize man make a "cute" face, but at this point Lewis still saw Daisy and the rest as women despite everything he had heard.

"It's different for everyone," said Edgar.

"Then tell me about you. They said you want to be here—"

"That's not true! I never said that," protested Edgar. "I'm here because of my wife."

"She sent you?"

Edgar blushed. "No... not quite. She was having an affair, and I found out about it. That's how I got here."

"You mean she was rubbing her affair in your face," said Bunny.

"And it was an affair with a woman," added Tiffany.

Edgar blushed even deeper and tried to ignore them. He spoke to Lewis. "She said she would stop if I came here and went through the program. She said it would make me a better man and then we could be together."

"A better *man*," giggled Cami.

"So you didn't know what they did here," stated Lewis.

Edgar visibly bit his lip. He hesitated.

"No, he knew," said Bunny. "His wife told him she wanted to wear the pants in the family and wanted to send him here to make sure he never could again. He agreed," said Bunny.

Lewis's jaw dropped. "You came here knowing what would happen?"

Edgar bit his lip and nodded his head.

"Well, I had no idea," said Cami. "My stepmother enrolled me."

"Why would your stepmother enroll you here?"

Cami shrugged his shoulders indifferently, which made his breasts bounce. Lewis assumed they were fake, but they were impressive fakes nonetheless. "You'd have to ask her."

"My stepmother enrolled me too," said Tiffany. "She told me that my father graduated from here from their boys program, and he would be proud of me if I graduated from the school too. So I agreed to enroll. Naturally, I had no idea what they really did."

"Why did she do that?"

"She's been fighting with my father quite fiercely. I kept taking his side, once too many times I guess. She decided she was going to get even with him by changing me. So when he went overseas for six months to run some subsidiary of the company he works for, my stepmother tricked me in to coming here. She even tricked me into keeping it a secret by telling me it was going to be a surprise for my father."

"He's going to be surprised all right," said Edgar sourly.

"At least I didn't agree to come here knowing what would happen," shot back Tiffany. This made Edgar burn bright red with shame and he dropped his gaze to his plate and wouldn't look up.

Bunny suddenly snickered cynically. "Well, I'm here by mistake, and I'm only passing through."

"What kind of mistake?" asked Lewis.

"My wife thinks I had an affair."

"Did you?"

Bunny avoided the question. "As punishment, she enrolled me here. I had to agree to avoid divorce, but it's only for one semester.

I'm done in a few weeks. Then I go home and everything goes back to normal."

"She's lying," said Edgar.

"She is not."

"She is. She just told you that to make you docile," argued Edgar.

"What would you know about it, sissy?" shot back Bunny.

Lewis had a million questions for each of them, but before he could speak, Miss Victoria came through the door and announced that lunch was over and it was time to return to class. She then ordered all the males to rise and form a line by the door.

As Lewis watched, one seeming girl after another rose to "her" feet and got in line. A couple of these could be young men in dresses, he thought, but not many. The rest had to be young women... sexy young women.

"They can't all really be men," said Lewis.

"They are," said Cami. "Every one of them. They're all boys. Everyone who comes here starts off looking like you, but ends up looking like Daisy."

Lewis shook his head. That was too hard to believe, wasn't it?

—o—

Evening finally came.

It had been a long and difficult day by the time Lewis was allowed to go to bed. Physically, he was exhausted. His feet and calves hurt from wearing the heels all day – heels they made him wear to bed for some reason. He had never worn heels before, so his feet and legs weren't used to them. What's more, he ran around on them all day with almost no breaks.

His ribs hurt from the corset. He'd never worn anything like that before either and Ms. Victoria kept it super tight all day to the point of making breathing difficult. It squeezed him constantly throughout the day. His testicles hurt too. The pain from the shocks had ended hours ago, but it was slowly replaced with a numbing soreness.

All told, his body wanted to sleep to recover.

His mind did too. His brain was trying to process far too much information, and it needed to sleep to do that. Right not, it was like the proverbial ten pound bag trying to hold twenty pounds of something. What was on his mind? Well, he was struggling with truly accepting the idea that he had been taken prisoner. Somehow, it all still seemed like a bad joke to him and he expected to be free in the morning. The cross-dressing/ feminization aspect of this was even harder to wrap his head around:

Why were they trying to turn him into a woman?

What did they gain?

Was Hunter crazy or was there something more going on here?

What exactly were they planning to do?

What was this "implant" that had been mentioned?

What would they do when no one came to claim him?

Did he actually look like a woman at all?

Why was this so humiliating and yet it

kept turning him on too?

These and a dozen other questions bounced around his mind almost randomly. And then he had more questions too. Were the other students in white dresses really young men? Everyone said they were, but this was so hard to believe. Where the others really young women? Why would you mix the two? And who would send a man here in the first place.

Most importantly though, he thought about what to do next.

Lewis considered what he had seen. He was in the middle of nowhere. The school seemed to be very isolated. There were only three buildings, but they were arranged in a way to keep him trapped inside, like a prison. Yet, even if he could get outside, the electric device would make escape impossible and the heels would make fleeing so very difficult.

"That's where I need to start," he told himself.

Lewis thought about various ways to yank off the device, but none of those would ever work. Not only was the metal too strong, but he would rip off his testicles if he tried it. He thought of various tools that might help too, but they all carried an even greater risk that he might end up castrating himself if tried to use any of them. He had a real problem.

"I need to figure out a way to get that *THING* off my dick! But how?"

There was only one way he could think of. The only way it was coming off was if they took it off for some reason. Presumably, they would remove it to fix it or clean it or something, right? That would be the moment he needed to escape. He would need to make a mad dash for the exit in that moment.

"That could be my only chance," he said.

Of course, that left the heels and some other issues in place, but that seemed to be the only way. He wanted to escape, but he didn't know how else to do it. All he could do was wait for the right moment and then make a break for it. In the meantime, he was stuck going along with their crazy program to turn him into a woman. That worried him a lot. And if the others truly were young men, then it worried him even more!

Chapter Six: "Discovery!"
—o—

Lewis awoke to the sounds of dozens of young women, er, men getting dressed and preparing themselves for the day. That meant high heels up and down the hallway, the rustle of skirts and lingerie, hair being brushed out and blown dry, and giggles. Lewis had hoped he would awake to find this had all been a dream, but that wasn't the case. He was still in the pink room. He was still bound in the corset. He still wore the heels. He still wore the cage. Nothing had changed.

Lewis rose from the bed and set his feet on the floor. They were still strapped in the high heels from the night before. They were sore. He tottered over to the door to his room and peeked out into the hallway. He saw silk and satin everywhere as the other young men moved about the hallway.

"They can't be males," he said again.

Lewis looked up and down the hallway at all their faces. Then his eyes went lower. His jaw dropped. Most of the students he saw wore panties or had already put on their skirts, but some of them had not. In those instances, he saw cages just like the one he wore! Indeed, at that very moment, Cami walked by with an enormous erection held prisoner inside *his* cage. Cami was a boy!

"Good morning, Laura," said Cami in his girlish voice.

Lewis swallowed hard. "Hi Cami," he said.

A moment later, Miss Victoria appeared and came straight to Lewis. She took him back into the room and checked the tightness of his corset. She actually tightened the laces slightly. Then she dressed Lewis in the white uniform dress again, and she led him from the building.

"Where are we going, Ma'am?" asked Lewis.

"We're getting you a complete wardrobe."

Lewis didn't like the sound of that. For one thing, he didn't want to wear women's clothes anymore. They were embarrassing. But even more ominously, there was no reason he needed a "wardrobe" unless Hunter intended to keep him here a long time. That, he definitely didn't want. Unfortunately, that wasn't his choice.

As they crossed the courtyard to the main building, Lewis struggled to keep up with Miss Victoria, who seemed to take a twisted pleasure in walking just a little faster than he could comfortably walk in the heels. She had already gotten about ten paces ahead of him.

This forced Lewis to move a little faster than he felt comfortable, which kept him on edge that he might stumble. On several steps already, he had nearly lost his balance or twisted an ankle. What's more, this increased pace caused Lewis to keep his eyes on the ground directly ahead of him so he didn't step on a rock or something and fall. As a result of this, he sometimes didn't see where he was headed.

As Lewis struggled to catch up, he ran straight into one of the instructors. He knocked three books out of her hands, which tumbled to the ground.

"Oh excuse me, Ma'am!" exclaimed Lewis with his head down.

He immediately crouched down and grabbed the books. As he crouched, he felt his testicles escape the tiny panties and swing beneath him between his ankles. He didn't know if his dress was long enough to hide them or not. He blushed bright, bright red.

"You need to watch where you're going, young lady," said the woman sternly.

"Yes, Ma'am. I'm sorry."

"What is your name?"

"Laura," said Lewis. He didn't want to call himself Laura, but he didn't want to get shocked either. He grabbed the last book and stood up straight to hand them back to the woman.

"Oh my God! Lewis?!" exclaimed the woman in a startled whisper.

Lewis's head shot up. His eyes met the woman's eyes. It was indeed his fiancée. "Maria!" he gasped.

Maria's head spun around to see who else was nearby. She spotted Miss Victoria coming back to retrieve Lewis; she had gotten about twenty steps ahead before she realized Lewis had stopped. "Pretend you don't know me, Lewis," whispered Maria aggressively.

Lewis nodded his head.

"Is something the matter?" asked Miss Victoria a moment later.

"We had a little collision, Miss Victoria," said Maria, "but it doesn't seem that anyone was injured." She took the books from Lewis.

"Well, that's good. This is our newest pupil... Laura," said Miss Victoria.

Maria laughed nervously. "Yes, we just met."

Victoria smiled politely at her and then told Lewis to follow her and "to keep up this time." She then continued her march to the main building where Lewis was to be measured for more clothes. As Lewis marched off after her, Maria stared in disbelief after him. How had he ended up here?

—o—

Lewis stood before the three-way mirror. He wore the corset, the cage, a pair of tight pink panties (with his testicles tucked inside them), the stockings and the wedge-heeled sandals. Around him, there was a beehive of activity as the school's seamstress and her staff measured every part of him and tried various pieces of clothing on him. They were talking to each other and Miss Victoria about everything they were making for him, but he wasn't listening. His mind was fixated on having run into Maria.

Part of him – most of him actually – was horrified at having been seen by Maria dressed as he was. She saw him in a dress and heels. *A dress and heels!*

"What must she think of me?" he asked himself.

There was a sick feeling in his stomach. This wasn't the type of thing one could just ignore or put past them. This was the type of humiliating moment that ruined someone's opinion of you. It stayed with you. He was sure she would see him in that dress and heels in her mind, couching down to pick up her books and then tottering away like some kind of pathetic child after Miss Victoria for the rest of her life. Every time they argued... every time they got romantic... every achievement he had as a man, she would see him through that emasculating moment. That is who he would be to her from now on.

"I don't think I can take that," he said.

Indeed, he suddenly felt a strong desire never to see Maria again just to avoid her judgment.

At the same time though, it was starting to dawn on him that Maria was the only person who could help him escape this... this... this whatever it was. For one thing, she was the only outsider who knew he was here. She also knew Hunter and her staff. If anyone could find a way around them, it would be Maria. Without her, he was doomed to stay here and be feminized.

"I don't want to be Hunter's dress-up doll for the rest of my life," he told himself.

Yet, this thought immediately added to his queasiness about seeing Maria again. Not only would she forever see his emasculation in her mind's eye, but she could claim to have saved him too. She could then hold that over him as well.

"I can't spend the rest of my life with her lording it over me that she saved me and her laughing about how I would have been some feminized prisoner without her! *Poor me, the damsel in distress.* I would never be a man again, even out of skirts," he whined to himself.

Lewis imagined Maria telling everyone how she saved him from a life in panties and he cringed. The embarrassment of that would kill him, and he had no doubt she would do it too. She seemed to have become more willing to emasculate him verbally in front of their friends of late for some reason.

"But would I rather be stuck here?" he asked himself.

He felt trapped. Even worse, he felt indecisive and unsure. Still, there was only one real answer.

—o—

Lewis was still struggling with his dilemma when Miss Victoria took him from the school's tailor shop to a room that looked like a salon or a makeup studio. The room consisted of salon chairs, mirrors everywhere and shelves and shelves of makeup. When they walked in, two students in white dresses and two in blue dresses shot to their feet and curtseyed to Miss Victoria.

"Laura needs to learn about makeup," said Miss Victoria to a woman in a pink smock who ran the shop.

The woman looked Lewis up and down, making him feel small, and then grabbed his chin and moved his head around so she could examine his face. "We should be able to achieve a very nice look," she said.

Miss Victoria thanked the woman and then left.

Lewis bit his lip. He didn't want to wear makeup any more than he wanted to wear high heels or dresses. Even the prospect of it helping him to perhaps "disappear" as a woman didn't make him any happier about it, not that he believed he could be made to look like a woman.

"Come have a seat, dear," said the woman.

The woman walked over to a table in the middle of the room. The table was covered in bottles and brushes and powders and creams. Standing on the table was a lighted mirror. There were two chairs side by side before the table. The woman motioned him to sit in one and she sat in the other.

"How much do you know about makeup?" asked the woman.

Lewis raised an eyebrow and said defensively, "If you're asking if I'm a sissy, I'm not. I've never worn makeup before in my life!"

"So you know nothing about it."

"Thankfully not."

The woman chuckled. "Then we have a lot to learn. Let's start at the beginning."

"I'd rather we didn't do this at all," said Lewis, though truthfully, the idea of being less obviously a man as Hunter and Miss Victoria kept him dressed like this did appeal to him.

"Don't worry, my dear. You'll love it by the time we're finished, and you'll feel positively naked without it!"

"Somehow I doubt that," said Lewis.

The woman grabbed a tin of powder and set to work. Over the next hour or so, she applied a basecoat to his skin, made his eyelashes longer and curlier and thicker, painted his eyelids, showed him how to use eyeliner and lipliner, painted his lips, and showed him how to color in the eyebrows that had been thinned so aggressively. And the whole time, she explained every single step to him.

"Pay attention, my dear. You need to know this."

"I'm never going to remember any of this," he told her.

"You will. It's just a matter of practice. You'll be back here every day for a week or so for further lessons before you start doing it entirely on your own. By that point, you'll be an expert."

Lewis shook his head. She had misunderstood him. He had no intention of remembering any of this or developing this "skill." If they wanted him in makeup, then they would need to do it to him themselves. "I can't see myself putting on makeup on my own," he said.

"Anyone can learn to apply makeup," said the woman.

"I don't want to learn it," shot back Lewis.

"You should reconsider."

"Why?"

"Because if you don't," said the woman calmly and without missing a beat, "we may need to go another route."

Lewis raised an eyebrow. "What do you mean?"

"If you won't learn to apply your own makeup, then we'll have to tattoo it in place so you won't have to."

"Tattoo?!" gasped Lewis. He had not expected to hear that! If they tattooed eye shadow or eye liner on his eyes or lipstick on his lips, he would never be able to present himself as a man again!

"Yes, tattoo."

"That's not possible!"

"Possible, yes. Preferable, no. But if you refuse to learn, then we will have no choice. Will we, *Laura*?"

Lewis had no idea what to say. The fact this woman had an answer so quickly and so calmly suggested to him that perhaps she was quite serious. Then, as if to emphasize her willingness to do things to his body that might be permanent, she pulled out four silver stud earrings from her drawer.

"Now sit back," she said. "I'm going to pierce your ears. Two in each ear."

Lewis's head was spinning. This idea of the tattoo, as emphasized by the pierced ears, really brought home to him for the first time that he was dealing with something potentially dangerous here. Up to now, no matter what had happened, he always assumed he could just remove the article of clothing, wash the dye out of his hair, or cut off the hated device and then he would return to being his old self, no worse for the wear. But now he got his first glimpse that some of the changes that were being worked here might be permanent changes that he would need to live with for the rest of his life, and which might force him to live as a woman.

He swallowed hard. This changed everything!

Lewis paid particular attention to the rest of the woman's instructions.

Chapter Seven: "A New Class Is Added"

—o—

COMPORTMENT: Students will learn to sit, stand, walk and carry themselves as proper young ladies. They will learn to walk gracefully in heels, to sit correctly in skirts of all lengths, and to carry their bodies in the most feminine of manners. Students also will learn to project submission and seduction through the art of body language.

— Femford School For Girls Catalog,
p. 9.

"We're adding a class to your schedule today," said Miss Victoria.

Lewis grimaced as he tottered after Miss Victoria. He didn't want more classes. He had enough to do already. Besides, each class meant further feminization and further humiliation. Unfortunately, there was nothing he could do about it.

"What class, Ma'am?" asked Lewis.

"Comportment."

Lewis froze. Comportment?! Could that be Maria's class? The prospect terrified him. Yes, he knew that she was his only hope to get out of here, but letting her see him like this would be utterly humiliating and having her as a teacher would be infinitely worse! He prayed it wasn't her class, but something told him it would be.

Another thirty feet and Miss Victoria turned into the classroom. Lewis pensively followed. As he walked through the door, he saw five or six students standing on one side of the room. The instructor stood on the other side with another student. The instructor was Maria.

Lewis swallowed hard.

"Here is Laura, your new student, Miss Maria," said Miss Victoria. "You already met him when he ran into you."

Maria smiled. "Ah yes. Thank you, Miss Victoria."

Miss Victoria left.

"Practice your pivots while I catch up with our new student," said Maria to the class. "Come this way, Laura." She never took her eyes off her feminized fiancé as she spoke.

Lewis nervously walked over to his fiancée. Her eyes seemed to absorb every inch of him. Lewis felt himself shrink moment by moment. It was intensely humiliating that she could see him like this.

When Lewis reached his waiting fiancée, Maria grabbed Lewis by the shoulder and walked him into the corner. He felt like a fool tottering into the corner in high heels under his fiancée's lead. When they reached the corner, she spun him around and glared into his eyes.

"What the hell are you doing here, Lewis?" she growled in an aggressive whisper.

Lewis was taken aback. He expected something a little more sympathetic.

"How did you even find me, Lewis?!"

"I— well—"

"Did you follow me? You had to. Why did you follow me?!" she demanded.

"I was, well, I wasn't sure— that is— I thought there might be someone else."

Maria's jaw dropped. "You didn't trust me? You thought I was having an affair and you came here to catch me? You little sneak! Well, it serves you right, Lewis. Look at the mess you've gotten yourself into now."

Lewis trembled. "You've got to help me!" he pleaded.

"I can't, Lewis."

Now Lewis's jaw dropped. "What do you mean?"

"What am I supposed to do, Lewis?"

"You work with them. Tell them who I am—"

Maria shook her head. "Forget it! If I tell them that I know you, they'll think I brought you here. Then they'll fire me and you'll be stuck here. No, we need to think of another way."

"But I need to get out of here before they do something... *something permanent.*"

"I get that, Lewis, but how?" Maria rubbed her temple as if she had a headache. "You've really screwed this up, Lewis. Why couldn't you just trust me?"

"I'm sorry. You got to do something though."

Maria took a deep breath.

"I can't become like these other sissies!" said Lewis. His voice betrayed his panic.

"All right, Lewis," said Maria unhappily. "I'm really angry at you for following me here. You've put me at risk by coming here even after I warned you. I should let them take you." She paused. "But I don't want my fiancé turned into a simpering sissy, so I'm going to help. I'll figure something out. In the meantime though, you need to go about your lessons as if nothing is wrong. Cooperate. No escape attempts. Nothing stupid."

"I won't, I swear," said Lewis.

Maria cocked an eyebrow. She was surprised he would be so afraid to try to escape. Then recognition appeared in her eyes and she looked down at his crotch. "Ah. You've been fitted with your device already, have you?"

Lewis turned an embarrassed red, but nodded his head.

"All right, so you realize you can't escape."

He nodded his head sheepishly.

"Ok. Don't try it, Lewis. Hunter isn't kidding. Also, you don't know me. Remember that. I'm just 'Miss Maria' to you. Got it?"

Lewis cringed. It was embarrassing that he was supposed to call his fiancée 'Miss Maria,' but he understood the need. It was important that Hunter not know of their relationship or she would work to stop Maria from helping him. He nodded his head and said, "Yes."

"Yes, *Ma'am*," she corrected him.

Lewis turned bright red with shame. "Really?"

"As long as you are here. Now say it."

"Yes, Ma'am," said Lewis and he felt a sick feeling in his stomach.

"Good. Now go join the other students. I'll contact you if we need to speak. Don't you try to contact me though."

Lewis curtseyed before he realized what he had done. His shame intensified. Then he made his way to join the other students. As he did, he realized he might need to do a lot of submissive things in her class. This was going to be difficult.

—o—

Vera walked into the small cafe. She wasn't sure why she was here, but she knew it was important. Maria never would have asked her to come all this way otherwise. She spotted Maria sitting in a booth wearing a dark raincoat and a black hat to cover her face. Her beautiful silk-covered legs were crossed and sticking out into the aisle.

"You definitely got mom's legs," said Vera.

"And dad's penchant for getting into trouble," said Maria.

Vera frowned. "That bad, is it?"

"Yeah... that bad. I need your help."

"Anything for my little sister," said Vera and she sat down. The two women ordered drinks which came a minute or so later. As they waited for the drinks, they made small talk. After the waiter left, they returned to the reason Vera had come all this way. "What's the problem?"

Maria took a deep breath. "It's Lewis."

Vera pursed her lips and furrowed her brow. She had never liked Lewis dating her sister. She saw him as unreliable and stupid. Also, having dated him herself first, she felt uneasy with him dating Maria. But, he was her sister's fiancé, so she tried to keep those thoughts to herself... at least a little. "What about Lewis?" she asked. Her tone barely hid her contempt.

"He followed me here."

"What a jerk! So you're worried he found out what you do for a living," said Vera sympathetically.

Maria let out a nervous half-chuckle. "Noooo. He knows what I do for a living now *trust me*... he knows it intimately."

Vera raised an eyebrow. "Is he breaking up with you?"

Maria shook her head. "No, it's not that," she said cautiously.

"What then?"

Maria cringed as she spoke: "He tried to get into the school. He thought I was having an affair and he wanted to snoop around to see if I was dating someone here. They caught him, of course, and they '*enrolled*' him."

"They 'enrolled'?" asked Vera incredulously. "Your fiancé has gotten himself enrolled? In the Femford School?"

"Yeah. They're putting him through the program right now."

The light of understanding came on in Vera's eyes with the power of a thousand watt bulb! Her face positively glowed. "*Oh. My. God!* You mean Lewis is prancing around the school right now in a cute little pink dress and terribly high heels acting like a little sissy girly girl?"

Maria blushed. "They changed the male uniforms to white from pink."

Vera's grin grew so large it looked like it might break out of the confines of her face. "Ha! So you mean Lewis is prancing around the school right now in a cute little *white* dress and terribly high heels acting like a little sissy girly girl?"

"I wouldn't have put it that way," said Maria in an embarrassed tone.

"I wouldn't have put it any other way. Serves him right, the jerk!"

Maria squeezed her sister's hand. "Vera. I need your help?"

"With what? Picking out a new boyfriend? I'll get on that the minute I get home," she said with a laugh.

Maria shook her head. "No. I need you to help me get him out."

Vera sighed. "Well, it was fun while it lasted."

"Will you please be serious?"

"I am being serious. What can I do? You know I don't work there anymore, and I never did have any influence with Hunter."

"You don't need any."

"Then how do I get him out?"

"He doesn't have a sponsor. You just have to pretend to be his sponsor and unenroll him," said Maria.

"Oh, is that all?" asked Vera snidely. "You want me to go back to the school and pretend that I'm his wife or girlfriend or something and ask them to pretty please let me take him home with me?"

Maria shook her head. "No. That will never work."

"Of course, it will never work."

"We need to be more clever."

Vera wanted to tell her that no amount of clever would help, but she had agreed to help her sister. The least she could do was hear her out. "All right, what are you thinking?" she asked.

"How about this? You pretend that he's your stepbrother. He was constantly bothering you about where you worked, but you never told him. One day, he rifled through your purse and found your last pay packet with the school address on it. He decided to check out the school all by himself without your knowledge. You only just found out what he did."

Vera considered this. "So now I want him back, is that it?"

"No," said Maria. "That won't work. They're too suspicious of him right now. They think he's some sort of journalist or investigator or something. You need to make it clear that you think he got what he deserves and you want him to finish the year at the school as punishment."

Vera chuckled. "And the fact I leave him at the school for the rest of the year is our proof that I really do want him feminized and that I'm not just helping him escape the mess he got himself into," said Vera.

"Exactly."

"Clever. Sneaky. But, um, do you really want him stuck there until the end of the year?"

"After a month or so, once they stop being suspicious, you come back and say you need him home to probate the will of a relative who died. They should be willing to let him go at that point, especially if you promise to keep him feminized and maybe even say you'll bring him back next year."

Vera smirked. "Or we can just let him finish the year. I could always use a maid."

"Vera," growled Maria.

Vera rolled her eyes. "All right! All right!" She took a deep breath and looked contemplatively into her glass. "It might work," she said finally.

And that became their plan.

—o—

Vera sat in Headmistress Hunter's office. She had been here many times before, but not for this reason or even anything close to it. She had already explained that Lewis was her stepbrother, that he was a bit of a jerk, and that he found the school because he was nosy. Hunter listened politely, but remained suspicious. She clearly thought there was something more going on.

"I was surprised when you called," said Hunter. "Lewis gave no indication of any connection to the school and he never mentioned your name. He wouldn't even tell us why he was here except for some obnoxiously false story about enrolling his daughter at the school."

"I was surprised when I discovered where he had gone," said Vera.

"I can imagine."

"You would not believe how angry I was when I realized what he had done. He had no right to look through my things," said Vera, "and even more, I was deeply embarrassed that he had come here. I worried that you might see this as a betrayal by me."

"Oh certainly not," said Hunter in a tone which struck Vera as Hunter actually saying, "Absolutely, yes."

"I really don't know what he was thinking," said Vera.

Hunter smiled politely. If Vera was looking for absolution, she wouldn't find it from Headmistress Hunter. Hunter protected the school zealously and she didn't like this at all.

Family members of former employees should not be invading the school. Besides, she still wasn't sure she believed all of what Vera said was true.

"Out of curiosity," said Hunter, "what does he do for a living?"

Vera shrugged her shoulders. "Last I knew, he worked at a parts supply company, but he may have been fired from that."

"He's not a journalist?"

"Lewis? Ha! Lewis is no journalist," said Vera. "He's far too stupid to be a journalist."

"He's not a private investigator, is he?"

"No, not Lewis."

Hunter took a moment to consider this. Her concerns still did not seem allayed. After a few seconds consideration, she raised an eyebrow and asked, "I suppose you wish to take him home?"

Vera saw the trap easily and shook her head. "Oh Heavens no! He made his bed, now let him lie in it. It will do him some good to go though the program... it will do me some good." Vera snickered. "I have to say that I do miss having these young men at my beck and call. It might be nice to have that again with Lewis when you're done with him."

Hunter smiled. This response made her happy. "And we will strive to make him exactly what you wish," she said. She opened her drawer and took out a packet of papers, which she handed to Vera. "I take it, you remember these?"

Vera smiled involuntarily, which made Hunter happy. "I do indeed. The 'in her image' sheet."

Hunter raised an eyebrow. "'In her image'? I'm not sure I heard that one."

Vera smirked. "God made man in his own image and woman remade man in her image. It's a little joke we used to have whenever we saw one of these sheets. Then we would tell the male how he was being remade to his wife's or girlfriend's or mother's specifications."

Hunter laughed.

Vera then finished her tea. "By the way, is there any chance I can see him?"

Hunter took another moment to consider this. Then she smiled. "Certainly."

Chapter Eight: "Checking the Box"

—o—

The visitors' room was essentially a library with several areas where groups of different sizes could meet. There were small tables with chairs on either side. Tables with chairs on all four sides and one table for eight. There were three areas with couches and coffee tables and three more areas with collections of soft leather sofas. The walls were lined with books and this part of the main building had floor to ceiling windows, like the lunch hall.

Lewis walked into the visitor room on his five-inch heels. He didn't like to admit it, but he was getting better at walking in heels every day. He was now quite stable in the wedges and his walk was moderately passable as a woman's walk, though he didn't realize his walk looked increasingly like a woman's. He just knew he was more stable. What's more, the training he was getting was beginning to develop a bit of feminine grace. He didn't realize that part yet either.

As Lewis entered the room, he saw Headmistress Hunter. He curtseyed as required. She motioned him to sit down in a high-backed chair. He did. As he did, he smoothed his skirt beneath him as he had been taught in Comportment, and he tucked his feet together beneath his chair. It was a very feminine move.

"I see you're coming along well, Laura," said Hunter.

Lewis blushed. "Yes, Ma'am."

"That's good. I take it you've given up any idea of escape?"

Lewis ran his tongue over his teeth. She knew escape was impossible, so why ask? She had to be rubbing in her control over him, thought Lewis. "Yes, Ma'am," he said coldly.

"Good. The sooner you realize that you will be our guest until your education is over, the better it will be for you. Unless, of course, you are a fan of unnecessary punishments."

"No, Ma'am."

"Well, in any event, I haven't called you here to chat. I've called you here because you have a visitor."

Lewis furrowed his brow. Who would visit him? Who even knew he was here? Suddenly, Lewis heard the sound of high heels to his left across the room. He looked to see who that was. There stood Vera in her elegant dress and devastatingly pretty heels. Lewis hadn't noticed her before. He saw her now.

His jaw dropped. *Vera!* he gasped to himself.

Vera slowly walked over to Lewis. Her heels tapped out her predatory-like progress which struck Lewis as a large cat stalking its helpless prey. She was smiling a wicked smile too. "You've been a bad boy, Lewis," said Vera.

"Laura," corrected Hunter.

Vera snickered.

"Why are you here?" asked the stunned Lewis.

"Oh, don't you know?"

Lewis swallowed hard. He couldn't imagine. Why in the world would Vera be here? Lewis and Vera did not get along. Lewis had dated Vera before he started dating Maria. They had had a passionate relationship, but it didn't end well. He dumped her, which devastated her. Then he started dating her sister Maria, which seemed to create a tiny bit of a grudge. Seeing her here now did not make Lewis happy in the least.

"I'm sure if you thought hard enough, you could guess why I'm here," said Vera. "How dare you sneak into my purse... steal my things... and then come here to what? Spy on me? What was your plan, *Laura*?" She really emphasized that name.

Lewis licked his lips. He had no idea what to say. "Um, um, well."

"Well, you made a mistake this time, *Laura*."

"I... I know."

"And you'll need to pay for it."

Lewis swallowed hard. Was this all an act? Was she trying to scare him? Would she say, "just kidding" any moment? Was she trying to fool Hunter in some manner? Or was she serious? How did she even know he was here? He was becoming increasingly confused. "P— pay for it?" he asked nervously.

"Yes. That's why you're staying her for the whole year... as punishment."

"Staying here?!" gasped Lewis.

"Yes."

"*The whole year?*"

"You wanted to see the place, now you shall."

"Do you know what they do here?!"

Vera took in Lewis's outfit from his high-heeled wedges to his stylish short dress to his perfect makeup with hungry eyes. She found herself getting wet. That didn't surprise her though, that used to happen to her all the time when she worked at the school.

Lewis felt himself shrink under her gaze. "I'd like to go home," he said like a child who could take no more.

"I want you here," said Vera simply.

Lewis shuddered. Was she serious? He understood none of this. When she walked in, he had hoped she was here to take him away. Now he had no idea why she was here or how she had even known he was here!

At this point, Hunter produced several pages from the sponsorship agreement forms. She handed them to Vera and told her that she needed to make selections about what changes she wanted made in Lewis. Vera, of course, knew this from her prior work at the school and said she would fill them out. She then took Lewis across the room where they could ostensibly sit side by side at a table and fill them out. In reality, this bought her a little privacy.

"Now stay calm, Lewis. Maria sent me to get you out," whispered Vera. Then she loudly said, "Let's fill this form out together."

"Maria sent *you*?"

"Yes."

"Why *you* of all people?"

Maria pretended to flip through the forms and tested the pen she had. "Because she trusts me. Now listen up. We have a plan—"

"Get me out of here now!" growled Lewis through gritted teeth.

"Not yet. We have a plan."

"You need to get me out of here *now*. They're going to start doing things that are... that are *permanent*!"

"Calm down, Lewis," said Vera.

"How am I supposed to calm down?"

Vera glanced over her shoulder and saw

Hunter and Miss Victoria chatting innocently. She knew this wouldn't last though if she didn't start filling out the forms. There was no getting around that. "We need to start working on this. Just go with it," whispered Vera.

Lewis furrowed his brow and didn't respond. He tapped his high heel against the floor angrily. "What is that?"

"It's a form they want filled out. It concerns your 'education.' I get to choose some special classes if I like and I get to request a few alternations."

"What kind of alterations?" demanded Lewis suspiciously.

"All kinds," said Vera. Her eyes skimmed down the page and she snickered. "So what do you think, Lewis? Would you rather be blonde or a nice Auburn?" She looked at him and chuckled. "I'm thinking blonde suits you best."

"Forget it."

She read another box: "Large firm breasts or *really* large firm breasts? Oh, I do like my men with large firm breasts," she said with another chuckle.

"That's not funny," said Lewis sourly.

"Oh look, Lewis. "I can check this box and have your balls removed."

"*Don't you dare!*" growled Lewis.

"Calm down. I'm only kidding," said Vera.

"This isn't something to 'kid' about. This isn't funny. I'm in real trouble. Why couldn't Maria come herself or send someone else? Why did she have to send her half-wit sister to help me—?"

Vera glared at Lewis. "Half-wit?! I'm not the one who got himself stuck in a girl's school, Lewis. And let me tell you, it's not smart to piss off the girl who holds all the power to decide what your future looks like. You treat me nice and you walk out of here with just a shave and a haircut. Act like an ass, and I'll have you turned you into Minnie Mouse or something."

"You wouldn't dare!"

"Try me," said Vera coldly. All the reasons she disliked Lewis so much streamed back into her mind. He was controlling, quick to anger and irrational when he didn't get his way. And the more she thought about it, the more she thought that maybe a semester at this school *would* do some good. It would eliminate all of the bad things Vera disliked about Lewis and which she didn't think Maria should need to live with. It would do Lewis some good too by making him a better man. He would be more like her own husband, who was kind, helpful and all around a great man to be with. That's what Maria needed, not this lout!

"Oh my God, this is perfect!" thought Vera.

"I could actually save Maria from making a huge mistake which would stick with her the rest of her life." She smiled at Lewis. Her smile made him shudder for some reason.

"What?" he asked nervously.

"I'll tell you what, *Laura*. Why don't you go back to class and I'll fill out this paperwork. I swear I'll do my best to get you out of here as soon as possible. Is that agreeable?"

Lewis took a deep breath. He realized that was likely the best he would get from Vera, so he nodded his head. "Yes, it's agreeable. *Just get me out of here*," he hissed at a whisper.

She patted Lewis on the silk-covered knee. "Will do, Lewis. Will do."

Vera waved Hunter and Miss Victoria over. She told them Lewis was ready to return to class and that she would fill out the form without him. Miss Victoria then marched Lewis back to class. In the meantime, Vera got to work on the form.

"When they're done with you, Princess, you'll be the perfect mate for my sister." She shook her leg excitedly and her nipples popped up. "Oh, did I say 'mate'? I meant 'maid.'" She became wet.

When Vera handed the completed form to Headmistress Hunter, Hunter was shocked at what she saw... very pleased, but shocked. Perhaps she had been wrong about Lewis being a reporter after all.

"Well, even if he was, he won't be when this is all done," she told herself.

Chapter Nine: "Starting The Program In Earnest"

—o—

Once again, Lewis found himself in the small clinic. The Rubenesque woman in the white labcoat and the thick heels motioned for him to take a seat. Lewis looked at the chair. It looked a bit like a dentist's chair only more sinister. Every instinct he had told him not to get anywhere near that chair, but he had no choice. He could not escape by running away. He knew that. And until he could win his release, he was powerless to resist anything they wanted to do.

So he slid into the chair. This time, the nurse strapped his arms to the chair. That was ominous.

"Good morning, Laura," said the doctor.

"Good morning, Ma'am," replied Lewis stiffly.

The doctor picked up the file and pulled out the forms Vera had filled out. "And what are we doing for you today?" she asked herself more than Lewis. She read through the forms and smirked. "You really pissed someone off, didn't you?" she asked rhetorically.

Lewis raised an eyebrow. "What do you mean?"

"Double-D... follicle transplant... chemical

cast— oh, look at that! Yes, you made someone very angry indeed."

"What are you reading?" asked Lewis nervously. He craned his neck to see the form, but couldn't reach. So he squeezed his butt cheeks to raise himself just a smidge higher so he could finally see over the top of the file at the form she was reading. It appeared to be the form Vera had filled out.

"Is that the form Ver— uh, my sponsor filled out?"

The doctor nodded her head.

"But— but she said she didn't want a lot of changes," said Lewis.

The doctor shrugged her shoulders. "I guess that depends on what you consider a lot. She seems to have given you the works though."

Lewis's jaw dropped. "That moron! She must have filled it out wrong!" thought Lewis. He sat up straighter. He needed to convince the doctor not to do whatever she was planning. "Um, doctor... uh, Ma'am," he said. "She honestly didn't want much done. She might have filled the form out wrong. She's not very bright. She could have checked the wrong boxes."

The doctor smirked. "No, this is right."

"But it can't be. She told me she wasn't going to order much."

"She lied," said the Doctor indifferently.

"But she said she wouldn't. She didn't want me changed—"

The doctor patted him on the cheek. "I'm sorry, dear. But this isn't at all uncommon. What she told you isn't what she wrote. She told you what was easiest to say face to face. But this," she said and she held up the signed sheet, "is what she really wanted for you."

Lewis saw the sheet clearly now. It was indeed signed by Vera and it had a lot of notes, a lot of comments, and a lot of checked boxes. "How could she?" he gasped.

"Like I said, you must have made her very angry. Look at the bright side though," she said comfortingly, "At least she's letting you keep your penis... tiny though it will be."

Lewis's jaw dropped. His head spun. He wasn't sure he had heard that correctly. Had she said he would get to "keep his penis"? Was that even an issue? This idea, that these women were doing something so intense, struck Lewis now like a ton of bricks. They really intended to turn him into a woman!

"Please, you can't!" he pleaded.

The doctor held up the forms. "Sorry, she's the boss."

A moment later, the nurse gave Lewis a shot in the arm. It started working almost immediately and he fell asleep.

Lewis awoke some time later. He didn't know if it was minutes, hours or days. All he knew was that he was in his bed in "his" pink room. He didn't feel much different at first. Then he noticed a soreness in his side. He sat up and examined it. He had two stitches, that was all. He also noticed that his face felt strange... kind of numb. He got up and examined it in the mirror. They had injected collagen into his lips. They were now large, puffy and feminine. His forehead seemed different too. There were now quite a few new short hairs at his hairline. The rest of him seemed unchanged though. He even grabbed his balls to make sure they were still there – they were.

"So was this all just to scare me?" he wondered. "No. They did do the lips. And they poked my side for some reason."

He checked his body again. There truly didn't seem to be any other changes. He had expected to wake up looking like the other sissies at the school, with flowing feminine hair, bouncy breasts and probably no penis. For some reason, he hadn't.

"I guess I dodged another bullet," he said.

Meanwhile, the implant began releasing the high potency hormones into Lewis's body.

—o—

Over the next few days, Lewis settled into a sort of schedule. He was awoken each morning, dressed and then went to breakfast. Afterwards, he went to class. They took a break for lunch before he returned to class. In the evening, they had dinner and then it was off to bed. The students went to bed early. He had no free time.

While this may sound like a typical life for a student, the truth was that his life was anything but student-like. Lewis spent his time constantly wearing dresses and makeup and high heels. He found this humiliating. He also found it somewhat painful. His feet were slowly adjusting to the heels, but they were still sore all the time. He was happy that he was adjusting, though he was unaware there was a price to that... a price he would soon discover. The corset seemed to get better every few days, but then Miss Victoria would tighten it again bringing back the discomfort. He assumed the corset was loosening over time, but that wasn't what made it looser. He would discover that soon as well.

The classes were ridiculous in his opinion. So far, he had learned to walk in heels, to sit in a skirt or dress without showing his panties, and how to carry a purse. He had also learned to make a bed, dust and clear a table while maintaining "feminine" posture – in other words, while looking like some kinky pinup. Even putting aside how embarrassing it was for him to be learning this, the whole thing struck him as incredibly silly. How did this make him a woman? All he had to do to ruin their plans was refuse to make beds when he got out of here, or change his posture slightly.

"This is not an effective program for whatever they are doing," he told himself.

That said, he did have to admit that the other young men did seem to be learning these things in earnest. That was their problem though, not his. He was ready to put all of this behind him the moment he got out that front door. He even imagined himself raising his skirt and mooning Hunter before he climbed back in his car.

That image made him laugh.

The thing that annoyed him most though was makeup. He was struggling to learn to apply his own makeup. The whole idea of wearing it was anathema to him and he hated the idea of feminizing himself in that manner. So he found it difficult to learn. It was only the threat of being tattooed which kept him working at it.

All told, the school was embarrassing, but seemed less threatening to him than it had originally.

—o—

OBEDIENCE: Students will further develop their submissive personalities by learning to reflexively respect all female superiors and to obey all commands from superiors without question or complaint.

— *Femford School For Girls Catalog,*
p. 16.

Today, Lewis would start a new class.

"Welcome to Obedience class," said Miss Caroline.

Lewis pursed his lips. "This sounds like dog school."

Miss Caroline seemed friendly enough. She was a small woman, even smaller than Maria with a childlike voice, who projected tremendous enthusiasm. She came across as perky and nice. But as she described what they would be doing with such glee, a sense of dread began to fill Lewis. The fact she held a riding crop doubled his fear. Then she made the point that this was an elective class chosen by their sponsors, which made Lewis angry. Vera had struck again.

"Now let's start with a volunteer. You,

Laura, you've just volunteered," said Miss Caroline.

"But I didn't raise my hand," said Lewis.

"Come to the front, Laura."

Lewis sighed. He didn't want to do this, but he did it because he had no choice. He rose to his feet and tottered to the front next to Miss Caroline. She smiled at him and then turned to the class.

"All right, class, tell me what Laura did wrong," she said.

The other seven or eight students, all boys, glanced around the room, but no one spoke up. This seemed to annoy Miss Caroline.

"Clearly, we have much to learn," she said.

One boy with long flowing Auburn hair and pouty feminine lips raised his hand. His nails were long ovals, painted silver. Miss Caroline called his name and he said, "Laura took her time getting to the front of the room."

"Yes," said Miss Caroline.

Another with yellow blonde hair raised his hand. "He didn't obey your order right away either."

"Correct," said Miss Caroline. "Everything Laura did showed resistance. It showed that she was not obeying me willingly, but only reluctantly. This class is about teaching each of you to obey the women in your lives as if it were your reflex.

Laura should have smiled and immediately agreed. She should not have sighed. Then she should have shot to her feet and come to the front with deliberate speed. Do you all understand?"

The other boys nodded their heads.

Lewis was less than thrilled that the other males seemed to be selling him out. He also wasn't thrilled that Miss Caroline seemed to be the first teacher to start referring to him with feminine pronouns. He hoped that wasn't a trend.

"So the fact Laura did not do this tells us that she still views obedience as optional. We need to fix that."

"Yeah, that's not happening," thought Lewis.

"So how do we fix that, class?" asked Miss Caroline.

No one spoke up or raised their hands. They just looked around nervously.

"We will teach Laura that actions have consequences. Obedience will bring reward. Disobedience will bring punishment," said Miss Caroline.

Lewis swallowed hard. He didn't like the sound of this. "How do we do that?" asked Lewis.

Whooooooooooosh THWACK!!

Lewis barely had time to see the riding crop as it flashed across his vision and cut through the air. It slapped hard against his exposed instep, and it stung. It stung so badly that Lewis almost went down to his knees. He didn't though, but his muscles did tighten and he did cringe.

"That was for walking slowly. From now on, Laura, you will walk with deliberate speed in my classroom. If you go slow or hesitate, I shall strike you again and again until you learn to obey me. Do you understand?"

"Yes, Ma'am," gasped Lewis.

The pain started to fade after a few seconds.

Miss Caroline moved around her desk and pulled out what appeared to be a thin plastic penis from a drawer. She held it up for Lewis to see. "As punishment for your attitude, I'm going to insert this inside you."

Lewis bit his lip. He had never had anything stuck inside his rear before, especially a dildo. "That?!" he blurted out nervously.

Miss Caroline shook her head. "What did I say about resistance?" She reached into her drawer and pulled out a thicker dildo. "I will now insert this one instead, because you again showed reluctance to following my order. Action, consequence, Laura."

Lewis swallowed hard.

"Now Laura, do you have any problem with me sticking this inside you?"

"No, Ma'am," said Lewis quickly and as

calmly as he could.

"Good. So bend over and grab your ankles."

"Right in front of all these other students?!" blurted out Lewis.

Miss Caroline set down the larger dildo and reached inside her drawer once more. She pulled out an even thicker one. "Action, consequence. Any more resistance and I shall use the fob. Understood?"

Lewis nodded his head. "Yes, Ma'am," he squeaked.

Lewis looked at the newest dildo. It appeared gigantic to him. Nevertheless, he took a deep breath and did as instructed. He bent over at the waist and grabbed his ankles with both hands. Behind him, he felt Miss Caroline spread some sort of gel on his rear. Then he felt the tip of the device toy with the edge of his crack. A moment later, Miss Caroline pushed the dildo through his hole inside of him. Lewis gasped. The dildo felt like it was the size of a tree and it felt like it was ripping him in half. He squeezed his ankles tightly and held his breath. His heart was pounding.

The dildo kept moving deeper.

Lewis was awash in feelings of pain, shock and discomfort. His rear felt like it was splitting in half. There was incredible pressure building inside him as if he would explode. How would this end, he asked himself nervously.

Then suddenly, the pain stopped. The pressure went away. The dildo had slipped far enough inside him that it entered some chamber and no longer pushed against his muscles. If anything, it actually felt kind of good. Indeed, he noticed that his penis was growing hard inside the cage.

"I think he likes it," whispered one of the other students.

This was followed by giggles all around the room.

Lewis shot them all a nasty look. "Shut up, sissy!" he growled.

"Laura!" gasped Miss Caroline.

Lewis cringed. He realized immediately that he should not have done that. He should have swallowed his pride and turned the other cheek, but he hadn't. Now he would pay the price.

"You will learn, Laura," said Miss Caroline.

"Yes, Ma'am," agreed Lewis.

Then, as Lewis stood there helplessly holding his ankles, Miss Caroline had each of the other students come up one at a time. They stood before Lewis and he was made to apologize to each and then perform as much of a curtsey as he could without releasing his ankles. They were then told to come around behind him and take hold of the dildo. Each would then slide it out several inches and push it back inside.

Lewis was utterly humiliated.

These eight young men each got a chance to pull on the dildo and then jam it back inside him. Even worse, they giggled the entire time like school girls, which made Lewis feel like he was on display, which of course, he was. Worse yet, the whole thing was making him uncontrollably horny and he found his erection throbbing whenever they manipulated the dildo. Each thrust was bringing him closer to cumming. If anyone ever found out he had stood there, bent over, as a group of young men played with a dildo in his rear, he would be humiliated for life!

When it was all over, Miss Caroline pulled out the dildo and made him return to his seat. His rear would be sore for two days after this as a reminder of the consequences of disobedience, it would take a lot longer for him to forget that this had happened. This was his first true lesson in what these women planned for him.

Chapter Ten: "It's Under Control"

—o—

Lewis spent the rest of the day and the following morning feeling highly embarrassed. He had the sense that everyone knew what had happened to him as if they could all see it written on his face: *hey, didn't you have a dildo shoved up your butt!* His anxiety over this made him nervous and sheepish. What's more, about an hour after the dildo was removed, his rear became very, very sore and that continued for a day or two. It served as an unwanted reminder.

That last thing Lewis wanted, as he dealt with his shame over the dildo, was to see his fiancée Maria again, but now that he had her Comportment class, he would see her every other day. The following morning was that other day.

"All right class, settle down," said Maria.

The collected young men all stopped their chatter and became silent. They curtseyed to Maria and then took their seats, each smoothing his skirt and crossing or tucking his legs as he had been taught. Each then put his hands together on the desk with his finger interlaced ready for class.

Lewis did this too. He had not been part of the chatter as he was still too embarrassed to speak to anyone. He also sat down much more gingerly than most. But he now sat with his fingers interlaced waiting for class.

"Today, we will learn to walk in mules," said Maria. "Fundamentally, mules are high heels and you are all familiar with walking in heels – though some of you are still wearing the wedges and not the stilettos yet. But mules present a special challenge to the wearer because of their lack of support, especially mules with only narrow straps over the toes."

"I've worn mules before," said Ginger after raising his hand.

Lewis glared at Ginger. "What kind of male admits that, even if it is true?" he wondered.

"Excellent, then I expect you to do well," said Maria. "Has anyone else worn mules before?" She looked around the room but none of the other boys would volunteer that they had. "What about you, Alexa?"

The boy with the curly raven-black hair shook his head. This made his earrings jingle. "No, Ma'am."

Maria looked around once more. She smirked. "Lewis. You've worn mules before. Tell us about your first time in mules."

Lewis turned white as a sheet. He had never worn mules before, so why did she think he had? He started to shake his head and sputtered out a response. "I've never... I swear!"

Maria chuckled. "All right, then come to

the front and we'll experience your first time together."

Lewis now blushed deeply. "Yes, Ma'am."

If there was ever a walk of shame, thought Lewis, this was it. He was walking to the front of the class, under the scoffing gazes and mocking looks of a half dozen other young men, so that his own fiancée could dress him in high-heeled mules. How could this get any worse?

When Lewis reached the front, Maria ordered another boy to come up as well. She gave this boy a key and told him to unlock Lewis's high heels. Lewis actually smiled at this. This would be the first time in days he had been out of heels. He didn't like that another male had been tasked with removing his shoes, but he was happy nevertheless.

The young man, named Wendy, got down on his knees and removed the first padlock. He pulled it out of the leather strap and the buckle. Then he unbuckled the shoe and he loosened the strap. At this point, Lewis raised his foot in the air and the young man slipped the shoe from his foot.

Lewis's foot was free!

Lewis set his foot down on the floor. It felt strange to have his foot resting flat on the floor. It felt oddly unnatural. It felt like it was straining to stay flat too. He'd never felt anything like this before. In many ways, it felt like when you stand on tiptoes. After a while, your feet become sore and your muscles strain to avoid going flat. This felt like that, only in reverse.

"That's just a trick of the mind," he told himself.

As Lewis watched, Wendy unbuckled and unstrapped the other sandal. Lewis raised that foot and Wendy pulled off his shoe there as well. Lewis then placed this foot flat on the floor as well. This one felt strange as well.

"Thank you, Wendy," said Maria.

Maria took the wedges from Wendy and set them on the desk behind her. She then grabbed a shoebox from her desk, one of many, and from it she pulled a pair of red patent leather mules. These had very high stiletto heels, being about five inches with no platform. The shoes themselves had little support too. Indeed, the only support was a leather band, about one-inch wide, which ran over the toes. She held them up for all to see.

"The classic mule," she said.

She then handed these to Wendy to slip onto Lewis's feet.

As Lewis watched this, he began to notice something odd. His feet were starting to hurt. It wasn't a serious pain yet, but it was growing. It felt to Lewis like when a muscle is straining as hard as it can and it slowly reaches the point of painful exhaustion. This was how his arms felt when he lifted weights in school and how his calves felt when he tried that marathon in college. This time, the pain was in his toes and his arches, with a tiny bit extending up into his calves.

"Why do my feet hurt from standing?" he wondered.

He pushed himself up slightly on his toes and discovered that the pain went away. That solved the problem. Then Wendy held out the first mule and Lewis slipped into it, to the extent one really "slips into" a mule. His foot felt better the moment he did. It was the same with the second mule.

"What does this mean?" wondered Lewis.

"All right, class," said Maria. "Pay attention."

She motioned for Lewis to walk from one side of the classroom to the other. He did as he was told, and he noticed right away that walking in these was a good deal more complex than walking in the strappy wedge sandals had been. The problem was that the shoe didn't come off the ground with his foot when he raised his foot, so it was easy to step out of them.

"You need to press with your toes," said Maria.

"Press with my toes?" questioned Lewis.

"Yes. Push your toes against the shoes to make the leather strap feel tighter over your toes. Then lift the shoe," she said. "Maintain the pressure until your toes are on the ground again."

Lewis tried again and it went much better this time: **CLICK SLAP! CLICK SLAP! CLICK SLAP!** Fortunately, he was becoming quite good in heels... if that could be called fortunate.

"Nicely done, Laura," said Maria.

Maria then instructed the other students to pick a pair of mules from the boxes on her desk and to get started. In the meantime, she walked Lewis over to the corner so they could speak privately.

"Nice work on the mules, Lewis. You're quite the natural in heels, honey. I'll have to buy you some when we get home again," she said with a snicker.

Lewis glared at her. "That's not funny." But his penis grew erect.

"How did it go with my sister?"

"Your sister is a dingbat," said Lewis.

"What happened?"

Lewis gritted his teeth. "She filled out the paperwork wrong. She was supposed to tell them to do nothing to me but maybe a haircut, but she told them to give me the works!" he growled.

"I'm sure it just seems that way," said

Maria.

"No. The doctor even told me I'm getting 'the works.' That was her word, not mine – 'the works.' Your sister is an idiot."

Maria furrowed her brow and licked her lip. "All right, I know you're upset, Lewis, but I don't want to hear you insulting my sister. She's helping us, after all. Keep that in mind."

"You might want to tell her what team she's on. Draw her a picture, that will help," said Lewis sarcastically. He was letting several days of pent up anger out at the moment. It was a mistake.

"Lewis," growled Maria. Her tone was a warning.

Lewis didn't heed it. "Seriously, she so is rock stupid—"

"Enough!"

"No! Not enough. You've let this stupid school go to your head. I'm your fiancé. I'm the man you're going to marry. I'm the head of the household. You obey me, so stop trying to order me around."

"Go stand in the corner."

Lewis furrowed his brow. "What?"

"You heard me, go stand in the corner," said Maria. "When I tell you that I don't want to hear you insult my sister, I mean it. Now go stand in the corner until I fetch you." She pointed to the nearby corner.

"You're not serious."

"Do you want to find out how serious I am?"

Lewis looked at the corner and then at his wife. "And what if I refuse?"

Maria reached into a small hidden pocket without hesitation. From it, she pulled the fob. She held it out for him to see with her finger on the button. "Don't try me, *Laura*," she said coldly.

Her tone sent a shiver racing down Lewis's spine. "She means it," he told himself. He gritted his teeth, swallowed his pride and nodded his head. "Fine... if that's what you want."

"Go."

Lewis slowly turned toward the corner and slapped his way over to it in the mules: **CLICK SLAP! CLICK SLAP! CLICK SLAP!** He felt intensely embarrassed. This has been his own fiancée who had done this to him and he could feel her triumphant eyes burning a hole in his back! He had been humiliated!

Maria, on the other hand, was feeling something a little bit different. She had discovered that she was already prone to feeling a sense of power when she ordered the feminized young men around. But to now order Lewis around was amazing. She had thought doing so would make her feel queasy or scared... but it hadn't. To the contrary, she felt even more powerful than usual.

What's more, she felt like this was the way it should be... the natural order of things. And as the rest of the class passed and she intentionally left Lewis staring in the corner, she kept looking over at him, wobbling in the mules and his dress blowing occasionally in the breeze, and she found herself genuinely turned on. It was true. She was turned on.

—o—

That weekend, Maria met with Vera again at the cafe. She wanted to find out directly from Vera how the enrollment had gone. She also wanted to get something off her chest. Both sisters wore red. Vera wore pants and pumps. Maria wore a loose skirt and sandals.

"How's Jay?" asked Maria.

"He's good," said Vera. She scrunched her nose. "He's home cleaning the house from top to bottom." Her tone was excited... gleeful.

"Is he really?"

"I needed to give him something to do to keep him busy, so I told him the place needed a good cleaning and he was to do every last corner on his hands and knees with a toothbrush." She giggled at the thought. "I even told him he should wear his little sissy maid uniform."

"He has a sissy maid uniform?" asked Maria incredulously.

"Of course. But I only let him wear it sometimes."

"You should have him clean my place when he's done," said Maria.

"Get your own sissy maid!" said Vera with a laugh.

Maria leaned in closer. "So Vera, tell me about the enrollment."

Vera shrugged her shoulders. "There's not much to tell really. Of course, Hunter remembered me. She was quite friendly about seeing me again. She seemed to accept the story too of how Lewis got there."

"Was she suspicious?"

"I would say she was. She definitely asked a lot of questions and it took her a while to accept my story. I think though the fact that I used to work there and that I got Jay from her program convinced her. Plus the fact I didn't try to get Lewis out right away."

Maria nodded her head. "I figured that would help."

"So, all told, it went smoothly so far."

"Did you fill out the consent form?" asked Maria.

Vera sipped her drink. Maria knew she had

filled out the form. She had to know. So clearly, her question was loaded. Vera played it cool. "Of course. I filled most of it out with Lewis sitting right there."

"Lewis watched you?"

"Yes."

"Lewis seems to think you filled in all kinds of changes." Maria let the sentence stop there and hover in the air rather than finishing the thought. She didn't want to accuse her sister of anything directly.

Vera calmly shook her head. "No. I gave it the minimum I figured Hunter would accept as legitimate, given the story we used. Now that's more than 'nothing,' but it's certainly not 'all kinds of changes.'"

Maria seemed satisfied by this. She then jokingly said, "So you didn't ask that he be castrated and turned into a giant nipple," to break the tension that her question had created.

"That? Well, yeah. I did do that, but that's nothing," said Vera also jokingly.

"I'm sure Lewis is just being paranoid."

"I'm sure."

Maria sipped her drink. "You know," she said in a more serious tone, "I hope this ends fast."

"I'm sure you do."

"It's been hard seeing Lewis at the school

every day." She didn't mention that Lewis was in her class.

"I'm sure."

"I almost lost it with him today."

Vera raised an eyebrow. "Really? Do tell."

Maria shrugged her shoulders. "He was just fighting me on everything. He kept insulting you," she said, which made Vera furrow her brow, "and I kept telling him to stop. He wouldn't, so I ordered him into the corner."

"You should have paddled him."

"Trust me, it was shocking enough that I sent him to the corner." She left out the moment where she threatened to shock him too. "The thing is... it was kind of... I mean, well, it shouldn't have been, but it was."

"Shouldn't have been what?"

Maria finished her drink. "Seeing him standing in the corner was kind of... *exciting*."

Vera laughed. "Oh Maria."

"What?" asked Maria in an embarrassed tone.

"You've taken your first step into a better world."

"I've done no such thing. I just made him stop being a jerk."

"No, you sent your powerless, feminized fiancé to stand in the corner like a little girl because he made you angry and it turned you on to do it," said Vera, putting a fine point on it.

Maria blushed. Then she grinned. "I wouldn't have put it that way."

"I wouldn't have put it any other."

The sisters giggled and ordered more drinks.

Chapter Eleven: "The Changes Mount"
—o—

Time moved incredibly slowly for Lewis over the next few weeks. It seemed like his stay at the school would never end. Each morning, he dressed femininely. Each day, he went to classes, had meals, and learned how to apply makeup. In the evenings, he returned to his room to sleep. One could almost say that life had entered a boring routine of sorts for him, except for two things.

First, at every turn throughout his day, Lewis found himself humiliated and embarrassed. Being seen by the others – especially the young women in blue – was humiliating. It didn't matter that most were in the same position he was in, the fact of being seeing dressed like a woman was simply embarrassing. And it was worse with the teachers. These were all gorgeous grown women. His ego told him he should be hitting on them and trying to get their attention as potential lovers. But instead, they saw him as a feminized toy, an ex-man on his way to becoming a submissive slave. That was deeply emasculating.

Even worse, one of these women was Maria.

His relationship with Maria was changing

too, of that there was no doubt. She was still trying to see him as "her man," the fiancé who would run their household when he finally escaped, but seeing him feminized every day and being put in charge of him was making it harder and harder for her to maintain the vision of him as man of the house. Consequently, little by little he was noticing her starting to treat him more like the other students. That scared him. It humiliated him too.

All of this prevented his routine from ever becoming boring.

The second issue was even more pressing. Between the training, the constant acting as a woman, the constant reinforcement of his submissiveness, and the medical efforts of the doctor, Lewis started to see changes in himself. At first, these were minor, but they grew fast.

For example, there was the ability to stand on tiptoes to alleviate the stress his toes and arches felt when he stood flat. This seemed like nothing at first – a solution to the problem of his muscles getting used to new types of work. But then he thought about what it really meant. Constantly wearing heels was slowly reshaping his muscles, and that couldn't be good. Sure enough, Lewis soon found it painful to walk flatfooted for very long; he couldn't imagine how hard it would be to walk any distance in flats. Soon thereafter, he started standing on his toes in the shower and whenever he was barefoot. He began to worry how he would jettison the heels when he left this cursed place.

Naturally, this changed his walk too. Even barefoot now, he found himself walking as if he were wearing heels. And when he wore heels, he didn't just walk, he walked seductively.

"I would give a room full of men boners," he told himself crudely as he watched his walk in the mirror one morning.

Then there was the corset. Every few days, Miss Victoria tightened the corset. Lewis had assumed that she needed to do this because his body motions loosened the laces that held it in place. Now he knew better. Bit by bit, the corset squeezed his body into a new shape. His waist had lost four inches and become hourglass in shape. At the same time, the hormones in the implant made his hips an inch wider and filled in his rear until it was pleasantly, femininely round. And that is to say nothing of his growing breasts!

"Take off your dress," said the doctor.

Lewis unzipped his dress and let it fall to the floor. He carefully stepped out of it, making sure not to tangle it in his heels. The doctor's assistant then took a tape measure and examined his chest. Lewis knew he wouldn't like the answer. He had already seen the evidence of breast growth. Not only had he seen it on the other young men, but his own chest had grown flabby recently to the point that the flab seemed to be forming into small round globes.

"Just beyond an A-cup," announced the assistant.

"That's a good start, but I'm thinking we'll still need implants to get to the double-D cups that his sponsor requested," said the doctor.

Lewis's jaw dropped. Vera had done this to him!! He knew it!! She had requested double-D cup breasts. Those were huge! They were even bigger than Maria's ample breasts. So much for asking for minimal changes!

"She's not going to get away with this," he swore to himself.

Lewis felt nauseas. Then he had a vision of himself kicking Vera in the butt. Only, he wore high heels as he did it... and he had enormous breasts. This vision made him tingle and he suddenly grew hard. This had been a problem of late for Lewis. For some reason, everything turned him on and he kept getting hard all the time. He was actually glad he wore the cage so no one else could see how turned on he constantly was, but he worried why this would excite him in the first place.

The nurse then strapped his hands to the chair and spread his legs. He knew what this meant. It meant they were going to open his cage to examine his penis. Binding his hands prevented any escape attempts while the cage was off, not that he considered escaping seriously anymore at this point. After all, how would he get out of here locked in high heels that impeded his progress, with the cage open but not removed, and nowhere to go? He would need to walk all the way back to town, several miles from here, and hope nothing happened to him along the way. That was not a prospect he wanted to face.

With his hands secured, the nurse unlocked the cage and opened it. Lewis's erection immediately popped out. She slid the tape measure along it, teasing him with the touch of her fingers to make it as hard as it would get.

It had been so long since Lewis had been able to touch himself that this felt incredible. He wanted more though. It had been so long since he came that he was desperate for her to make him cum. She would not do that, however, so he had to settle for the tingly warmth of her touch.

"Down one-half inch," she announced as she read the chart.

Lewis shuddered. He saw his fate in those numbers if Vera didn't act soon. His erection apparently was half an inch shorter than it had been before they started the hormones. No wonder the cage didn't bother him as much.

"I need to get out of here!" he exclaimed nervously inside his head.

The nurse measured his balls next and noted that they were smaller as well.

The doctor then brought over what appeared to be something straight out of *Star Trek*.

"What is that?" asked Lewis.

"This is a laser," said the doctor.

"What are you going to do with it?"

"We're going to remove your hair."

"Like shaving?"

The doctor shook her head and snickered. "Not quite. This works on the roots. When this is done, you'll have silky smooth, hairless skin and you won't need to shave." She pointed the device at his throat and she pushed the button.

"For how long?" asked Lewis suspiciously.

"This is permanent."

Lewis felt a shudder tear through him. The hair transplant surgery had given him a feminine hairline, which was growing in nicely... for a woman. And now he would get a face to match... and a chest... and legs. They would even remove the hair around his penis. Add in the breasts and the shrinking penis and he had problems. Indeed, if he stayed here any longer, he wouldn't be able to go back to being a man!

Lewis cursed Vera.

Chapter Twelve: "A More Important Change"

—o—

Maria watched Lewis smooth his skirt, sit down and throw his leg over his knee. He popped the stiletto pump off his foot and let it dangle like an expert. Then he brushed back his hair with three fingers on one hand. He looked utterly feminine and, truthfully, that made her wet. She didn't want it to excite her, but it did, and that brought her a sense of shame, which made her want to deny that any of this excited her.

"I'd like to see you over here for a moment, Laura," said Maria.

Lewis uncrossed his legs. He put his feet together. Then he rose and he tottered across the classroom to her: *CLICK! CLICK! CLICK! CLICK! CLICK!* It was an utterly feminine display.

When he reached her, he curtseyed. It humiliated him, but Maria had started requiring it lately. Ostensibly, she didn't want him standing out from the others, but deep down, part of her got a kick out of seeing it.

"Yes, Ma'am," said Lewis.

Maria cringed at his increasingly feminine voice. This change was coming from a class he was taking called "The Feminine Voice." At times, this change excited her, but right now she felt the opposite because she felt guilty at being excited by the changes in him.

"Do you have to talk like that?" she snapped.

"I'm sorry, Miss Maria," said Lewis in the feminine voice.

"Stop it."

"I'll try," he said in the same voice. This seemed to spark a moment of anger within Maria.

"Honestly, Laura, can't you fight any of these changes? I mean, good God, look at you!" She brushed his hair with the back of her hand and then grabbed his breast and squeezed it through his dress. "You're practically a girl already. And then you saunter in here on high heels like you've worn them your entire life. You sit like a sissy. You talk like a sissy. You're becoming a sissy! I don't want to marry a girl, Laura," she said harshly.

The truth, though, was that she was feeling tremendously confused. Seeing Lewis feminized was turning her on. She didn't want to admit that because it meant she could never be happy with macho Lewis when he got out of here again, but it was true. That made her sad, it made her angry. Why had Lewis ever followed her here?! Why couldn't he fight the feminization better than he had?

Lewis opened his mouth to speak, but Laura cut him off.

"Go to the corner," she growled.

Lewis turned without question, the result of his "Obedience" class. This only made her anger worse. He hadn't he even tried to resist her. To her mind he should have said: "I'm your fiancé, forget it. You don't control me!" but he hadn't. This angered her.

"Get back here," she snapped.

Lewis turned around and returned to her.

"Grab the desk," she said.

Lewis wasn't sure why she was so angry, but he wasn't going to fight her either. He knew what she wanted. Others had wanted it before her. She had never done it to him, but she had the right as a teacher. He spread his legs, leaned forward and grabbed the edge of the desk with both hands. Meanwhile, Laura grabbed a long black rod she kept in the corner. She gave it a test swing.

Whoooooooooooooosh! It cut the air.

Then she changed her mind. She wanted to feel his rear grow hot beneath her hand to know what she was doing to him. She stepped up along side him and raised his dress over his rear. Then she pulled down his panties, exposing his butt. She pulled back her hand and let fly. It came down hard on his rear.

SMACK!

Maria felt the blow in her palm. It felt good actually... cathartic. She raised her hand and let fly again.

SMACK!

Once more, she felt her palm strike her fiancé's rear.

SMACK!
SMACK!
SMACK!

She struck him again and again. She felt such release striking him like this. All of her frustrations and fears and guilt seemed to be leaving her with each blow. At the same time, Lewis felt smaller and smaller with each blow.

"Should I really allow this?" he asked himself.

"She's my fiancée, I should tell her 'no'!" he told himself.

"Why am I letting her humiliate me?"

And yet, he did. He let her strike him over and over, humiliating him in the process. His fiancée had spanked him as if her were a little child.

Maria finished. She stood up straight again. Then she pointed to the corner. "Now go stand in the corner."

Lewis did as he was told.

Maria watched Lewis totter to the corner on his heels. His rear swayed as he went. As she watched this, she was overcome with an image of her and Lewis at her apartment. Maria sat on the couch, reading a magazine. Lewis was moving around the apartment... cleaning. He was wearing a corset dress and high heels. He wore no panties. His penis was hidden behind the cage. Maria could feel the fob which would let her set off the device if she wanted, though she hadn't needed too. Lewis had become too docile to offer resistance.

"It was a long day," said Maria.

"I'm sorry, Miss," said Lewis.

She pointed her stockinged foot at Lewis. "Rub my feet."

"Yes, Miss," said Lewis. He set aside the broom and tottered over to Maria. She savored the sound of his heels against their hardwood floors. The heels symbolized control to her. When he reached her, he dropped to his knees and took her warm, soft foot in his hands. Her foot was still sweating from being in her pumps all day. That didn't stop him though. He started massaging her foot with his hands and it was glorious. His touch sent waves of pleasure racing up her legs and made her pussy wet.

"You do that well," she said. "But aren't you forgetting something?"

Lewis blushed. Then he leaned forward and slipped her smelly toes between his lips and into his mouth. This made Maria's pussy positively tingle. She was becoming so horny. She shifted slightly so she could raise her other leg and she placed her other foot on the cage. Lewis could feel the warmth of her foot radiating through the cage, but he couldn't touch her flesh.

"Maybe I'll let you out tonight if you're a good boy," she said.

She rubbed her foot against the cage and played with his testicles with her toes. She could tell she was driving him crazy, but there was nothing he could do about it except suck her toes harder.

She laughed. Then she pulled her legs away and spread them.

Lewis knew what he needed to do. He moved forward, slipping between her thighs, extending his tongue.

Maria giggled. Her giggle snapped her back to reality and she realized that some of the students were looking at her strangely. Her face blushed. Then it dawned on her what she had been fantasizing about and she really began to blush!

"What does this mean?" she asked.

The End of Part One.

Thanks for reading my book!
I hope you enjoyed it!

Please sign up for my newsletter!

Get news, updates on new books, captioned images, author interviews, and more.

You can also win free books.

All you need is an email address. Sign up here:

https://annmichellebooks.wixsite.com/website

You can see a sample newsletter here:

https://mailchi.mp/d81fa5f2218c/october-newsletter

Don't forget to check out my other books. The complete list is at my Amazon homepage:

https://www.amazon.com/Ann-Michelle/e/B007JLQ9RG/

—o—

Blackmailed Sissy Maid

Powerful men like Christopher Jordan need ways to unwind. For Christopher, who planned to run for governor in the next election, this meant having a safe, anonymous internet mistress. But this mistress wasn't as anonymous as he thought. Christopher would now learn a hard lesson as this mysterious mistress slowly placed him at the mercy of the women in his life.

August 2013 No. 1 Best Seller in Transgender Erotica at Amazon!

—o—

Caught By His Roommate

Mitch thought Katie was the perfect woman. She was beautiful. She was innocent. She was naive. And best of all, she dressed the way young women should dress in heels and dresses. So Mitch tricked Katie into becoming roommates so he could explore her closet. Unfortunately for Mitch, Katie would catch him red handed. That's when things got really strange for

Mitch. See, Katie wasn't as innocent and naive as he thought, and she had plans for her new sissy!

June 2017 and July 2017 No. 1 Best Seller in Transgender Erotica at Amazon!

—o—

Caught In Her Closet

Jimmy always enjoyed cross-dressing secretly when no one else was home. Then he gets caught by Christine and her friend. What will Christine do with her new stepsissy?

June 2017 and July 2017 No. 1 Best Seller in Transgender Erotica at Amazon!

—o—

A Collection of Short Stories, Volume One: Three Tales of Halloween Magic

They Messed With The Wrong Witch: Three rotten brothers learn a lesson they will never forget when they wrongly accuse a woman of being a witch.

The Magic Ring: A husband and wife argue over a magic ring only to discover that magic can be a dangerous and tricky thing. Soon they learn what happens when the shoe ends up on the other foot.

I Wasn't Myself: The tale of a man who finds himself in the body of his ex-wife. That's not the worst part though. The worst part is that his ex-wife is now in his!

—o—

A Collection of Short Stories, Volume Two: Tales of Feminization By Hypnosis

Save Us Sis!: Candice gets a plea from her brother to come save him and their father. Is this a joke? Or is something sinister going on at home?

Controlled By His Roommate: Dave is about to learn that his roommate Katie has more control over him than he thought!

The 'Disappearance' of Alpha Mu: A college committee investigates the 'disappearance' of Alpha Mu fraternity. Though, 'disappearance' might be the wrong word.

Hypnotized Husband: Diane is shocked when her husband starts dressing like a woman after he participates in a hypnosis stage show. But all may not be as it seems.

September 2018 No. 1 Best Seller in Transgender Erotica at Amazon!

—o—

Dress Coded

Written in the spirit of *Grounded in Heels*, this is the story of Charlie Mitchell. Charlie wants to wear shorts, but the dress code doesn't allow it. He tries it anyway, figuring that the worst the principal can do is

send him home for the day. Boy, was he wrong!
Before he knows it, Charlie finds himself stuck in
skirts and dresses and worse. What will the other
students think? Will this complicate his run for class
president against his nemesis... Stephanie Mills?

*May 2018 and June 2018 No. 1 Best Seller in
Transgender Erotica at Amazon!*

—o—

Emasculating My Husband

When I married Mike, I thought I had found my fairy-
tale prince. He seemed to be strong and confident
and the kind of man you wanted to lead the family you
hoped to build. Sadly, I soon learned that he was
none of those things. Still, I did my best to be the
submissive little housewife I had been taught to be.
Then one day, just as I could take no more, I came
upon a hormone cream that would change everything.
Before my plans were finished, Mike would be the
submissive little housewife in the four-inch heels!

*June 2015 and July 2015 No. 1 Best Seller in
Transgender Erotica at Amazon!*

—o—

Femford School for Girls (Part One)

Lewis Stevens thinks his fiancée is having an affair at
the secretive girl's school where she works. He
decides to sneak into the school to find out. Little
does he realize that this girl's school has another
purpose. Now he finds himself trapped and going

through their program. Can his fiancée help him? Will she want to?

May 2017 and June 2017 No. 1 Best Seller in Transgender Erotica at Amazon!

—o—

The Femford School (Part Two)

Each day Lewis remains trapped at the Femford School, he finds himself feminized further. Bit by bit, his masculinity is being stripped away. What's more, Vera has set into motion a series of changes that will forever alter Lewis's mind and body to make him Maria's submissive pet. Only Maria can save him now, but why does she keep dragging her feet? Can Lewis resist long enough to convince her to save his manhood?

June 2017 No. 1 Best Seller in Transgender Erotica at Amazon!

—o—

Feminized and Cuckolded

Junior Executive Brent Jones watches as their new boss Rebecca seduces and marries his friend John. Before Brent's very eyes, she begins to feminize his friend. So why doesn't Brent do something to stop her? Well, it's complicated. See, he wants her for himself, and if John's a girl, that might make it easier. This can't end well.

April 2017 No. 1 Best Seller in Transgender Erotica at

Amazon!

—o—

Feminized By His Mother-in-Law: Part One: Not Man Enough

Christopher has a problem. He has a beautiful new wife who loves him, but his mother-in-law thinks he's not man enough for her. Even worse, she's set out to prove it. Can Christopher stop her from making him not a man at all?

February 2018 and March 2018 No. 1 Best Seller in Transgender Erotica at Amazon!

—o—

Feminized By His Mother-in-Law: Part Two: Not Woman Enough

Christopher's problem is getting worse. Not only is his mother-in-law still determined to prove that he's not man enough for his wife, but now his wife is starting to think she wants him feminized. Can 'Chrissy' escape his increasingly feminine fate?

March 2018 No. 1 Best Seller in Transgender Erotica at Amazon!

—o—

Feminized By Hypnosis

Jess and his stepmother never got along, at least until she brought him a new CD. Now they get along great, and Jess and his father are changing fast. Everyone seems to be noticing the changes too, except them. Can Jess's mother save Jess and his father from his evil stepmother? Or are they destined to become sissy maids... or worse?

September 2012 No. 1 Best Seller in Transgender Erotica at Amazon!

—o—

Feminized Cuckold

When powerbroker Paul Jackson loses his job, he finds himself at the mercy of his trophy wife. Little by little, she feminizes Paul as she turns him from domineering husband into submissive housewife. She even invites his former best friend to move into their home, and she cuckolds him. Will this be his new life or can he escape his fate?

September 2012 No. 1 Best Seller in Transgender Erotica at Amazon!

—o—

Feminized Fiancé

When Victoria Martin built 'The Martin Firm' into one of the most prestigious firms in the world, she expected that her daughter Sarah would one day follow in her high-heeled footsteps and take over the business. When she learns that Sarah is planning to marry a young man Victoria considers entirely unsuitable, however, Victoria sets out to make sure Sarah will never want to marry him... by turning him into a woman.

November 2013 No. 1 Best Seller in Transgender Erotica at Amazon!

—o—

Serving His Fiancée (Part Two of *Feminized Fiancé*)

Rick is now trapped in a rigged bet with the powerful Victoria Martin. Rick must win his fiancée back to regain his freedom or he'll be trapped as Victoria's sissy maid forever! Complicating Rick's plight, Victoria is forcing him to masquerade as his fiancée's personal maid 'Sissy', and he can't tell her who he really is. But does she already know?

January 2014 and February 2014 No. 1 Best Seller in Transgender Erotica at Amazon!

—o—

Feminizing Her Husband (The Complete Story – Parts 1 & 2)

Part One: How Megan Avoided Pregnancy: Megan and Mark can't agree. Mark wants a baby, but Megan does not. When Mark issues an ultimatum to his wife demanding a baby, she counters by demanding that he dress as a woman for nine months before she will agree to get pregnant. Naturally, she assumes her macho husband will never agree. Imagine her surprise when he does. What follows is a cat and mouse game as each tries to trick the other into giving up.

Part Two: How Megan Got Pregnant: Things are changing fast now as Mark begins to 'grow' into the role of 'Princess.' But Mark isn't the only one changing. Megan is about to undergo a major change as well. Will Mark get the baby he wants? Will Megan let him escape with his masculinity intact?

May 2016 and June 2016 No. 1 Best Seller in Transgender Erotica at Amazon!

—o—

Grounded in Heels

When Sam's stepmother discovers the perfect way to keep her stepson out of trouble, she unknowingly puts him at the mercy of his worst enemy... his vengeful stepsister Diane. Now Diane has plans to make sure he never escapes. Can Sam find a way to save himself or will his summer in heels become a lifetime sentence?

April 2013 and December 2015 No. 1 Best Seller in Transgender Erotica at Amazon!

—o—

Grounded In Heels (Part Two: Back To School)

With Sam's stepmother forcing Sam to return to school as 'Samantha' until she can find a way to undo the feminine changes Diane has done to his body, Sam must learn to deal with being a young woman surrounded by the people who knew him as Sam. Can he keep his secret? Even worse, Sam still finds himself under the absolutely power of his vengeful stepsister Diane, who has plans for the helpless feminized Sam and is determined to humiliate him and to make his time in heels permanent. But her plans might now work out so well this time.

December 2015 and January 2016 No. 1 Best Seller in Transgender Erotica at Amazon!

—o—

Her High-Heeled Solution

John's wife Suzie wrongly thinks she's caught her husband having an affair. With the help of a friend, she comes up with an ingenious way to guarantee that John will never have another affair: she locks him into a pair of high heels. This simple solution goes wrong, however, as husband and wife both try to outwit each other. Soon events are spinning out of control. What's more, standing in the middle of all of this is Crystal, Suzie's best friend, who is having a grand time manipulating them both to make sure John gets slowly feminized.

November 2015 and December 2015 No. 1 Best Seller in Transgender Erotica at Amazon!

—o—

The House On Femford Hill

Would you stay in a haunted house? What if the house was known for turning men into women? Professor Eric Meyer plans to stay. See, Professor

Meyer studies the strange, the supernatural, and the paranormal, and he can't wait to investigate the famed House on Femford Hill, which is rumored to turn those who stay overnight into women. Could this be true? Professor Meyer intends to find out.

October 2018 No. 1 Best Seller in Transgender Erotica at Amazon!

—o—

Humiliation At The Office

For too long, corporate hotshot Andrew Boden treated the women of the office like sex objects. Now his secretary is out to settle the score as she slowly feminizes him and traps him in an inescapable web of femininity and humiliation. Little by little, Andrew loses his power, his freedom, and his masculinity, and everyone at the office is noticing.

March 2012 No. 1 Best Seller in Transgender Erotica at Amazon!

—o—

The Making of Danielle (Parts One Through Five)

This is my take on a very classic idea that comes up often in our genre: the idea of the young man transformed by an evil "Aunt." Daniel is an unruly young man who fights constantly with his stepmother. To end the fighting once and for all, his stepmother sends Daniel to an Aunt he's never met who will teach him discipline. Imagine his surprise when he finds himself put into skirts and he is trained to become a girl.

November 2016, December 2016, January 2017, February 2017 No. 1 Best Sellers in Transgender Erotica at Amazon!

—o—

The Making of Danielle, The Illustrations

The Making of Danielle series is now illustrated! It took almost a year to complete that project, but it was well worth the wait. All told, there are thirty images total across all five books and they are amazing! Drawn by Andy from andysdames, the images tell the story perfectly! They are well worth adding to your collection.

June 2017 No. 1 Best Seller in Transgender Erotica at Amazon!

—o—

The Story of William, From The Making of Danielle

This is the story of William and how he was transformed into Wilma. These are the things Daniel never knew. *It is also the conclusion to Daniel's story.* How does Daniel's story end? In a word: a wedding. To whom is the question though!

June 2018 and July 2018 No. 1 Best Seller in Transgender Erotica at Amazon!

—o—

Miss-ing Billionaire

Reporter Martin Ward has uncovered an incredible story. The billionaire founder of Ing Co. is missing, and Martin's source tells him the billionaire's new wife is behind it. Unfortunately, the only way Martin can investigate this story is to disguise himself as a woman. Can he do it? Should he do it?

August 2016 Best Seller in Transgender Erotica at Amazon UK!

—o—

More Than He Bargained For

Jeff wanted to change his wife. He wanted her to be more adventurous in the bedroom, so he took a long shot on some hypnosis tapes. Only, she found out what he was doing. That's when she decided to teach him a lesson he would never forget by giving him exactly what he wants and so much more. His life at home and at the office will never be the same. (This includes the alternate cuckold ending as a bonus.)

March 2013 No. 1 Best Seller in Transgender Erotica at Amazon!

—o—

My Femdom Marriage (Part One)

This is the true story of how my wife took over our

marriage and made me her feminized slave.

March 2018 and April 2018 No. 1 Best Seller in Transgender Erotica at Amazon!

—o—

My Femdom Marriage (Part Two)

This is the rest of the true story of how my wife took over our marriage and feminized me.

May 2018 No. 1 Best Seller in Transgender Erotica at Amazon!

—o—

My Lactating Husband (Part One)

What would you do if you started growing breasts? That's the problem Andrew faces. His life was great. He had a loving wife and a good job. He was even up for a promotion. Then he took an experimental treatment meant to grow hair... but something else grew instead. As his chest slowly expands into a pair of classic breasts, he finds his wife taking over and himself demoted. What's more, his boss wants him to report to work as a secretary! Where will this end?

September 2018 and October 2018 No. 1 Best Seller in Transgender Erotica at Amazon!

—o—

My Lactating Husband (Part Two)

Things are really headed in the wrong direction now for Andrew. Not only can he no longer hide the "growths" on his chest, but now he needs to report to work as a secretary... dressed as a woman. Even worse, his new boss is not exactly the nicest woman. How bad can she be though? Andrew is about to find out. Hopefully, he can remember the things his wife taught him about being a woman.

October 2018 No. 1 Best Seller in Transgender Erotica at Amazon!

—o—

Satin Falls (Part One)

Satin Falls is the story of a small mountain town where the males slowly lose their ability to resist any command given by the females after an unknown virus infects the water supply.

July 2015 and August 2015 No. 1 Best Seller in Transgender Erotica at Amazon!

—o—

Satin Falls (Part Two)

With all the men of Satin Falls now infected by a virus that causes them to lose their ability to resist any command given by any woman, the women of Satin Falls take over. Following Dr. Melanie Morgan's plan, the women remove the men from positions of authority and then feminize them for their own good. Unfortunately, none of them yet suspects what Melanie is really up to.

August 2015 No. 1 Best Seller in Transgender Erotica at Amazon!

—o—

Short Story: The Magic Journal

After macho football player Brad ruins her date, Rachel gets even using a magic journal which lets her change his body as she wishes. Brad is about to learn a lesson in feminization he will never forget.

—o—

Summer in Skirts (Part One: Becoming Summer)

Paul is sent to spend the summer with a crazy old acquaintance of his parents. He's not too happy about it either. Making matters worse, he finds a pair of twins already living there, and they have designs on him. They seem to think he should be obeying them. Naturally, he has a different view on the matter. Before long, they teach him the meaning of petticoat punishment. Things go increasingly more wrong – or right – from there.

July 2018 and August 2018 No. 1 Best Seller in Transgender Erotica at Amazon!

—o—

Summer in Skirts (Part Two: Queen of the Fair)

Now that Paul is firmly stuck as 'Summer' for the rest of the summer, it's time he explored his new relationship with the wonderful Ellie. Unfortunately, the twins are about to take center stage in his life again, and Paul isn't going to escape them this time. Ellie has a plan, however, but Paul isn't going to like it.

August 2018 No. 1 Best Seller in Transgender Erotica at Amazon!

—o—

Two Weeks As His Wife's Feminized Submissive

Paul Wallace is a powerful man. But Paul has a secret. While Paul appears to be a man in charge, his wife Amanda really holds the power. What's more, for two weeks every year, Amanda turns Paul into Paula, her feminized, submissive plaything... and he loves it.

November 2016 No. 1 Best Seller in Transgender Erotica at Amazon!

—o—

Wager Into Womanhood (The Complete Story – Parts 1 & 2)

Max is an arrogant sexist with a submissive wife and an inability to turn down any bet. Will is a househusband with a dominant wife who just caught him having an affair. Both of their lives are going to change significantly when they get tricked into entering a bet to prove that they can live as women for a week... or longer.

September 2017 No. 1 Best Seller in Transgender Erotica at Amazon!

—o—

The Writer's Secret

Loren had no idea what he was getting into when his agent suggested he write transvestite fiction. Nor did he realize how eagerly his wife Stephanie would embrace the idea of feminizing her husband. How far would they go?

March 2012 and October 2015 No. 1 Best Seller in Transgender Erotica at Amazon!

—o—

The Writer's Secret (Part Two: Blackmailed Sissy)

As Loren continues to adjust to living as a woman, his life becomes complicated when a young relative of Stephanie's comes to stay with them. This seemingly sweet and naive young woman turns out to have an unexpected dark side, and a penchant for blackmail. At the same time, Stephanie faces a boss who demands that she sleep with him if she wants to keep her job. How will Loren and Stephanie get out of these messes?

September 2015 and October 2015 No. 1 Best Seller in Transgender Erotica at Amazon!

Made in the USA
Columbia, SC
11 May 2023

16487957R00098